The Timid Leaper

D1640641

BLAST PRESS IMPRINTS

The Timid Leaper

inner nature poems

Gregg Glory
[Gregg G. Brown]

Writers Club Press
San Jose New York Lincoln Shanghai

The Timid Leaper
inner nature poems

Writers Club Press
an imprint of iUniverse, Inc.

For information address:
iUniverse, Inc.
5220 S. 16th St., Suite 200
Lincoln, NE 68512
www.iuniverse.com

ISBN: 0-595-23097-0

Printed in the United States of America

"Tiou, tiou, tiou, tiou—Spe, tiou, squa—tio, tio, tio, tio, tio, tio, tio, tix—Coutio, coutio, coutio, coutio—Squo, squo, squo, squo—Tzu, tzu, tzu, tzu, tzu, tzu, tzu, tzu, tzi—Corror, tiou, squa, pipiqui—Zozozo-zozozozozozozo-zozo, zirrhading—Tsissisi, tsissisisisisi-sisis—Dzoree, dzoree, dzoree, tzatu, dzi—Dlo, dlo, dlo, dio, dlo, dlo, dlo, dlo, dlo—Quio, trrrrrrrrrr—Lu, lu, lu, lu, ly, ly, ly, ly, lie, lie, lie, lie—Quido didl h luly-fie—Hagurr, gurr, quipio—Coui, coui, coui, couri, qui, qui, qui, gai, gui, gui, gui—Goll, goll, goll, goll guia hadadoi—Conigui,   horr,   ha   diadia   dill si—Hezezezezezezezezezezezezezeze couar ho dze hoi—Quia, quia, quia, quia, quia, quia, quia, quia, ti Ki, ki, ki, io, io, io, ioioioio ki—Lu ly h le lai la leu lo, didl io, quia—Kigaigaigaigaigaigaigai guiagaigaigai couior dzio dzio pi."

—*Transcription of a Nightingale's song made by a French Composer*

"A mouthful of earth to remedy all."

—*Edward Thomas*

Contents

THE TIMID LEAPER

Contents

THE SWORD INSIDE

Contents

CONSTELLATIONS IN DECEMBER

THE SOFT ASSAULT

Contents

DISSEMBLING EARTHS: ADDENDA AND A CONCLUSION

Foreword

This iUniverse book is a first for BLAST PRESS. This sort of combined electronic publishing and on-demand item, done with a higher quality might appeal to any number of BLAST PRESS readers. I hope this inaugural collect of four poetry books finds an audience to enjoy them.

Our other titles are available at the price of $2.50 per item, which includes shipping. Email me at **gregglory@aol.com**, or visit **http://www.corporategreed.com/gregglory** for more information.

See the back of this book for titles and quotes from other BLAST PRESS offerings.

Preface

Catastrophes and Trophies
Report from a Victor and Victim

This collection is actually the combination and slight rearrangement of four separate volumes of verse; almost all of these poems were written in the calendar year 2001. It's not much to show for a year of human life—that rich mystery we are twisted into by such a resolute hand. The main emphasis of this collection (as I hope will be quite clear) is Nature. Nature and Naturalism are not quite the same thing, however, and I have always had my own disagreements with the various proponents of those who took too dogmatically Thoreau's painful premise "Simplify, simplify, simplify." The Timid Leaper sets the keynote of this mixed approach. I hope this collection achieves some grace while trying to attain such goals. It is the beauty of man's reach exceeding his grasp. The Timid Leaper leaps, not from any discernible goal he might attain, but from some more subtle cause, some interpenetration of events that defies analysis and germinates poesy. The sub-title is "inner nature poems," and that is to help show that the weather for humans is never merely a matter of what's over our heads—it's what's in our hearts as well.

A victim of depression during the composition of these verses, I noticed an inability or unwillingness to assign purpose within myself—I was lax and ready to suffer unmitigated disasters with little more than a shrug and a tear. This is really a rather hopeless state of affairs—as a number of the poems outline. I remained staunchly impressed, however, with Dame

Nature's capacity to excite the recognition of meaning within myself. As meaningless and adrift as I may have been, I could not help but notice that Nature still evoked in me the wry acknowledgement of a more masterful hand in the pictures I kept seeing—both before me and within me. "No Wood to Sing Through" shows the adaptability of natural instincts and impulses. It was inspired by my observation of a catbird still thriving without its native habitat, and by my own reflection that I was seeing something meaningful—even when my depression had revoked my self as any inherent source of meaning. Something was helping meaning to survive even in the brain of someone who refused the acknowledgement of meaning. Something in me wanted, at least, for meaning to survive—or, more exactly, for the expression and acknowledgement of meaning to continue happening, despite my conscious wishes. This is a form of nature's nurturing weather—it is harsh and humbling. Can't I be meaningless if I want to? Don't take that shred of self-definition away from me! But, opposite of Sartre perhaps, it seems that meaning remains contiguous with essence, even when that essence wishes to exile meaning. It is this co-created weather of inner and outer that is charted in this volume of verses.

Full of wily wit and a bastard's bavado, The Sword Inside was the first burn and purge preparing a place for a new self to take up residence. I had to be rid of old hopes that I had harbored too long. Hopes are the white lilies of the soul, and when their time is past, they fester as fast. There were reconciliations to be made here as well, and rueful acknowledgement followed hard upon the heels of aptly rapid self-wit. Well-rooted weeds and lingering things were burned out, or hacked at with a saber, Some villany of habit and temperament had to be acknowledged and integrated, a black sheep returned to the fold. Such traceries of whim explored and displayed in The Sword Inside were the iron rungs I used to clamber back from the void.

The section entitled "The Soft Assault" stands apart for its being the documentation of a very severe personal storm—and so shows the purely human side of the weather. Nature purists and vegans of nature poetry may safely skip this section if they do not want their nature poetry too irredeemably mixed up with the human roots of that poetry in the poet. This section is the fever chart of one of love's bitterest victims. The natural phenomenon of the "inner weather" gives these poems their place in this collection. My retreat into nature, and nature's "soft pursuant touch" of my capacity to keep seeing meaning no matter what, are a direct result of the catastrophes alluded to within these poems.

Indeed, it was nature's "soft pursuant touch," that I could not shake off, and that led me back to myself as more than a recording barometer of outside events. Nature creates great art, but she uses dirty fingers. Soon enough, I was actively pursuing designs and meanings of my own in the material that had fauceted upon me. I was ready to assign parts to clouds and prompt the trees with dialog. When this hubris expressed itself too heavy-handedly, the poems themselves rebelled—and those poems have been expelled from this collection as a complete botch. But,—as I now think significant,—I was saved. And more than saved, I had become a victor from being a victim. Out of my personal catastrophe, I have extracted this volume of verses, which will serve as well as anything for a trophy.

Gregg Glory
[Gregg G. Brown]

Chronology

This quick collection saved my life.

May 20th—July 28th 2001

The Timid Leaper

The Night Orchard

Petal falling followed falling petal
Till all apple trees held was sky above;
Such a burst of sweetness discharged from air
Put mind out of reckoning for its cares.
We walked laughing through the snowing grove
Whirling the fallen in splashes back up,
Widening soft confusions in our wake,
Chapleted in blossoms that all spring throve,
Like trees ourselves glowing with tree-petals.—
Earth and air to a fantastic whiteness blown,
Shining as puddles from yesterday's shower.
Yet trees, for all their loss, did not look to be sad.
To rely on having is to be had.
New leaves yattering new green to new leaves
Talked for all the world about the breeze,
As if blossoms had kept them quieted as snow
And, having shaken off their winter calm to play,
They did not know what to say or know
And so said everything in a single day.
Evening found them standing solemn with the stars
Thinking how little they were themselves
Beneath bright things hung up so far.

Starlight cast down starlight like sky decayed.
All the night orchard stood restored to blaze
As if no single petal of them all
Had suffered earthward a single fall.

The Wind Trees Keep

Trees that have it in them to be a wood
Gather dark thoughts where bare hilltop stood.
Branch to branch entreats, and root goes out to root
Entangling dirt with movement deliberate
As worms, and mix their living sinews
With cold dead earth, its coldness to renew
And above the burning hilltop bring
A shadowy wing never alighting.
Starless night hovers where noon once reigned
And exiles grass, and laughing feet detains
With extricating minuets of wait
And then pass on,—a guardless garden gate
Forever shuddering in the wind trees keep,
Murmuring night-long while the world's asleep.

The Black Pony

A pony came whose coat was black as pitch,
Whose blood was broody as water in a ditch.
Her eyes were saucers of red command,
Her teeth grew square on the taste of hands.
Wildflowers grew more wild at her passing scent;
Like nerves through skin she raced where she went.
There was more than strangeness in what made her so.
There was more of night in her hooves than men know.
Proud, unobeying breed of tameless hills,
Storm of strength with a godless guideless will.
What light burned behind her being may
Not have been heaven sent, but burned to stay.
An inner star served as her only lamp:
None took her, none kept her, none triumphed.

The Old Quarry

The old quarry's flooded echo came back
To him almost exact, but left a blunted blank
For song, a lack of deadened cold echo
In so much dank; the quarry air was too
Soft and queer to sough a song out right,—
Yet still the listening stone, it seemed, white, uptilted,
Knew that song might be meant, to judge by crevice
And shadowed device and looks that meant no peace
Nor gave advice beyond the dusty tans
Rained down on singing man. One saw then,
The quarry was all quivered walls and rocks
A mocking water swallowed at the bottom.
It resembled nothing so much as a tomb.
Man's voice rolled all against the abandoned lot,
Echoing himself his repeated tune again
Like nothing else in nature that to voice pretends;
He was his own superior echo then
While song pursued its end as if never begun,
And time dilated some in jarring after-echo,
Or made itself felt as one,—as dark burns on in coal
While fire unfolds fire. Here, some soft after-noise
(As in the mare the moaning foal) made some alloy,
Forging voice and form alive in the willful quarry
To totter and rejoice alone where dead water stayed,
—A second singing voice came from bland clay,
And was heard some way. It seemed, for once,
The offence of voice had persuaded voice
To once not stay remanded in veined marble
But grace half-garbled, but half-audible,

The silent singer's startled ear, and speak
Some talk of the theme he'd followed half-awake
Into the choked dark of the watery quarry.
What he caught of what came back made him wary.
"I won't be sorry. I won't, I won't—"
He straightened up half-sighing, as if he'd meant
Never to hear his own want in song he'd given
All his graven morning to, and that, if spent above,
Would have vanished less riven into eve
Than the grave day that the quarry gave.

Two-Edged Liberty

Liberty has two edges still,
One to keep free, one to kill.

Strokes

Clear-headed time at a touch
Shows all too much.

The resentful body grows old;
Youth and strength have gone
Disgraced from the stage.
Vague as a notion,
The room swims into view;
Dawn stutters into motion.

Time has done to you
Things time shouldn't do.

An old man stares out
From an oval steel mirror,
Your face in one clout
The face of a stranger:
Cataract-eyed, his blind
Grip gone round a razor.

The Thrush at the Sill

Bright beyond belief the morning sun
Presents a double blazing image
Above the sink, bewitching just enough of dawn
For me to throw both windows back in homage.
I went forgetful about my round of chores,
Touching openness neither less nor more
Than I was bid by my round of chores.

Sunset had sun exit as it had come,
In doubled glory. A thrush burst out at once
Loudly loud, as if woods and house were one
And eaves leaves.—And thank, yes, forever thank
Such song for how it came and its coming in
To wake indoor woods beside my sink.
Thank thrush for landing home in homing in.

A Late Milking

The upper pasture gate creaked padlocked.
A wading lantern to show the latch
Flared where invisible things attach,
Carrying light snatched up for open use
To home a tricky key and save a curse.
To burn out opposing night and burn day back,
And give dark description where words must lack,
Light's concern was kept narrow as the lock.

At a click, light soon waded on to earthy dark,—
Swung wondering in a guideless hand
Familiar with the black of pasture lands;
Sudden cow or knoll indifferently stood stark.
I followed from below as I was, restless
To see how aimless light in darkness does.

The Broken Boxcar

At an unsteering speed of stoppage,
Detourned from straight tracks and wages
Into a listless field gone over
Mostly to pale thick-blossomed clover,
A boxcar keeps still its steel rails
Going both ends nowhere in parallel.
At the blackness of the door
A bandit gathers gold once more,
Pulling yellow raspberries
From some single spray above the weeds,
Reaching the rarewire richness
With nimble hands and quickness,
Palming sunset tears from thorns;
The racoon drinks them one by one.
Nothing comes to the rusted hitch
Clawing air above a gopher ditch,
No iron hand arrives to steer
And with knuckled coupling make a pair,
To clasp its open mate from the clearing
Into a sky of tear-streaked stars
Where time would hoist a husky boxcar
From its slatted stall and decay
To paradise, all the way.

Yet in the eye of a ruffed robin,
On her hopeful nestful throned within
Where the red roof caves in
From leakage and mineral rain,
Glints a hint of levitation—

In her high eye alone it seems
A flying boxcar bursts with wings
Like eyelashes; below it, everything
Lies amiably disordered,
Earthbound and solemnly sordid,
While heavenly visitors to her nest
Feed her safe chicks, and she rests.
So much of vision came to eye, and awed.
A unpersuaded caw cawed
From the litter of the field
The hunching crow refused to yield,
A black bold spot that picked for trash
In weeds gone bright to whiteness.
Now only time, for what it's worth
Flying still on its changeful path,
Turns the structure in its soft clutch
Like a moody sleeper back to earth.

Lakeside Sketch

Where a single steeple keeps the sky
And a scribbled wet of charcoal darks
Laps lapsing to meet the day,
—Crosshatched by wind's artistic lark,—
Monday quiet's come, as quiet may
Upon one meditation-taken;
After-silence serves some way
For all the echo left the lake.

The boathouse goes down to dock
On knees of battered pilings.
Suppliant to greet common rock,
The dock goes flat as filings.
Astute, the musing rock
Lets the mirror water watch
What it has mind enough to mock:—
Searchers who seek a latch.

There is no back or access side
To such a thing that is all is;
And if you say *inside*,
And take inside out to see what 'tis,
I'll say, 'tis better far to glide
Whatever offered surfaces
And decode what pleasure there resides
In such interstices

Than creep through dark, however wide
The open crosshatch seems or is,
To pull apart, to peer at tides

Whose motives are their business,—
And trouble them enough alive
To wash our prayers with their sighs.

Something Like

I longed for something something like too long.
My ablest eyes had two ears of seems—
Each tree I heard, I heard shake some human song;
Two eyes never looked but I saw two stars along,
No weather raved but trailed some inner storm.
My analogizing mind knew but what it deemed.
Nothing brought what it had meant to bring,
No shape manifest but in related form.
Of what I'd been gifted I got nothing, no thing.
Alone in life's simulacrum I saw or heard
Less than one third of every third's third.
All my blessings blessed transformed.
Ready at last to be, no matter being's marr,
I'm satisfied with sighing *is* and *are*.

Something Put

Like the flower near at hand I grow
Upwards by light into all I know;
Buried in ignorant dirt by a downward thumb
I bend dumb beneath rain into what may come.
Like a flower in summer now I grow tall,
Concentrate a seed out of all I've been,
Put half my something into that seed to fall,
Drop it unseen on wide ground, and then
Name that something put my all.
Is that something put experience gathered in?
Or is ignorance all when any all begins?
My ignorance decides me—I cannot tell
What seed, in growing there, may yet become
Besides new ignorance beneath the sun.

The Burning Anvil

My breast is a burning anvil
Cannot hammer a likely shoe
Stern enough to trace unglued
A racing lifetime through and through.

My breast is a burning anvil
Full of causal smokes and coughs,
More than youth at times had thought,
Between hammer and anvil caught.

My breast is a burning anvil
That sparks with the loss of heat
When edge and edge, hard and hard, compete
To shape each and each to mate.

My breast is a burning anvil
Cannot cease to pause or cool,—
As industrious, dedicate a tool
As any I'd forgot I forged.

My breast is a burning anvil
Full of tragic din and error
As any beating thing that mirrors
The hotness of my terror.

My breast is a burning anvil
Cannot pound out a likely star
As real as evening's first clear
At whose clarity I stare.

Timebends

Something about where the pebbled path in day
Splits, or in evening even trines,
Makes me wonder about the purpose of the way.

How many must have used their footsteps just to come,
And in coming here pass on in time,
As if all wheres we go are comparable to when.

And yet, time's a path more linearly ordered,
One whose steps will not divide,
No matter at what shady banks or grasses we loiter—

We may not, cannot, no matter how tried,
Reverse the going flow, or, breaking it, abide.

Snaps

How small a snapshot lies in hand
That held such grandness in its lens.
A perspective granted only *once* and *when*.
What we see of what is just depends.

Bounded by a regular white of lack,
I look at the detailed littleness;
A thumb occludes a mountain in the west
Like a painter perhapsing a sketch on scrap.

Snapped charm of vistas that had turned my head,
Develops charms of Time new-enlisted
To re-focus a moment visited.

Out of the frame winces one of my dead;
I turn the flat for date, and recognize
How loss and tears consume what's snapped by eyes.

Prisms

A spider, web, and alderberry bush
Arranged December in a quiet crèche;
The spider's stitching straw was soft and fine
As anything that ties us to the divine;
An afternoon of hidden breaths condensed,
Strung with dew as if of dew composed,
A blazing cobweb out of cold mist—
Dew-prism looked on prism, all in all,
And saw summer's wonder from before the Fall
Until every thread of light was put out by the loss
Of sun. Twilit dews sparkled into frost.
Each gentle juncture hardened to a cross.
Stiff additions of still more strength and grace
To dropleted water, by increments erased
Weave's living give and left a stony place
To which the chapel spider was not accustomed.
A rigid web in an alderberry niche,
Still and silver as a collection dish.
From her holy central belly it spiraled out,—
A frozen wheel or prayer-mat to invite
Chilly fervors of the not-yet devout.
You couldn't think such religion altruistic,
And could only thank it if a mystic
And believed all troubled birth a pause
Between our cyclings back to Cause.
The spider didn't think it mercy, that's certain.
She rushed behind her tautened curtain
To lay a landed fly into her winter stock
And knit the praying fly a little silver lock

That has only a mystic key.
She sought to bead a new dew to see,
Since day had gone blinded down to night,
And one more dark into her web was caught.
But even a spider with her sticky tricks
Can find occasion to make a slip
On such transparency gone slick;
The icy wire and her dainty claw-tip
Met without resistance, though her weight was there,
And that gave a tumbled feeling of unfair
And brought spider slipping past the fly
Who looked at her with all of his eyes,
Gave an inch leap, and was gone.
The diamond web with ice was diamonded.
The spider threw a line to save her pride
And back toward the frozen center slid.
She poised unpleased, ready for dark dispatch,—
A philosopher at a damaged treasure-latch,
Meditating what Fate might have brought
In the richness of the fly near-caught,
And then what wealth of blood denied,
The treasure chest a blank inside.
Perhaps the spider, if she had tried,
Might have persuaded the praying fly
He'd be in for blessings if he died.
(Too bad he'd already taken off on his
Aerodynamic errand or business.)
Wheels within wheels and layer upon layer.
Death would rank him up a rung,
Nearer You and I as human beings
—Or *two* rungs up. Yes. To convince the buyer,
Persuades more than a hundred prayers,
Thought this spider to herself, cool and sly.

But there was no nimble buzzer skating by
To heed the sales-pitch of the spider,
Save those flies already saved inside her.
With eight great eyes and eight great arms,
And well-equipped to deal out harm,
She resumed half-folded her coldly central position
As ready for Fate as anyone
Defeat had bruised and brought
Hungrier for what she had not caught.

Iris Vision

It's been a well-worn
Year since my iris has gone
Whose dark-headed heightened grace
Had tripleted heart's pace
And made the threatening waters
Irradiate the lighter
For her being something darker.
She brought her blue-black laughter
Like an aftereffect of thunder
When lightning rare as wonder
Makes a landscape dark as murder
By its too-much light, and, lighter,
Touches earth and sky together.
Now the garden, disused and mossed,
Grieves green, and I am lost
As rain that runs away,
As a thought that will not stay,
Or childhood song that refuses to play.
My iris in her wonted place,
Sensed through broken mist and lace,
In tree-shadows lifts her face.—
I see her here returned,
Nor may I this wish unlearn
As long as dew in dawn's-light burns;
Every shady curl of worth
That my flower had leased from earth
In sable richness reappears,
Full of rampant ribbon-shapes,

Taking all of root and stalk
To reach to light, and, silent, talk.

Unmask Us

I come to stare at leaves as deep as snow,
That have sent the roots to sea, that know
A restlessness I, restless, know.
I come to stare at leaves as deep as snow.

I turn the rake, send tines upended
Not to use as I intended
But to lean and stare as if deep in snow
And hear the restless things I know:

Too many things put aside or shunted
That had been centered when I started,
Too many things a life must ask us,—
So quick a quiet moment will unmask us.

A moment's thought, and all disguise
Resolves itself into surprise;
A moment more of wonder, even more,
And ignorance the disguise restores.

Leaves unsheltered by the coming wind
Rub the half-bare trees where they began;
They move as they would there once again
Climb to be leaves returned by wind.

Deep behind the mask, a whisper knows
There's an old hole of light to show
Just where we've come, and yet may go,
Among restless leaves as deep as snow.

Conscience Is Grass

My conscience is grass surrounding every side
Whispering, whispering. No help, no guide.
When I at last lie down, it will lie by my side,
Never saying do or go, but only: be, abide.

The Wounded Woodsman

I passed a knoll and passed it every day
Along the same soft deserted loam
Until a track as bare as bone
Followed along my way.

It was in its going I saw it first:
Narrow willows in a lovely copse
Where the wounded woodsman lops
The last to lay with the first.

I had not noted the knot of wood,
Or taken the view to do myself good—
Although the fresh-cut white of the willow-ends
Made some temporary amends.

–[Versioned from Edward Thomas'
   "First Known When Lost"]

Boardwalk Bonfire

Build the storm-brought wood till its right to burn
—A civilization, an amended word;
Completion and destruction turn
A dead-end rhyme as mated words.

The long matchstick cracks, a broken finger,
A wail to salt the self-subsuming wood;
—As if no injury could make ginger
Our conscience to aid the good.

I know myself, and play my hand
Shadowless in the flame and briny fire
Until a new pink hurt like stinging sand
Bids hand withdraw, and I perspire.

A Summer Prayer

All our hours vacillate
Like summer clouds gone sliding by
Clotted, vein-veiled and late,
Froward or deadly shy
Apparitions of the empty,
The essentially empty sky,
To dissipate in an hour's downpour.
All our hours, all our hours.
Our most famous nimbus
And more hallowed halo are
Our only blessings, bare and lent
By God, devil, or doubtful goal
In dance of dread amusement.
Each day we eat and ache,
Something dark for its own sake
Laughs at our glittering fate;
We tend our hours like a wish,
Alone but for some softer guess—
Our heart-happiness uncertain
As divinity's parted curtain.
What remains of marvel here
Of all that drifts to dust
Beneath a sky irremediably clear
Is the irascible particular;
The him of him, the her of her.

Listen to the wind and to me—
Let lending lend in leniency
An open, ageless, real reprieve

(In which unsafe hearts may yet believe)
To all our human tenancy
Defined by that proscenium
Under which we're born and moan
Full of voice and softness,
Full of whispers and of curses.
With the individual soul,
—With that and that alone,—
Wherever soaring moves above
Or going goes in having went,
Be thou communicant.
And this as well I wish and say
To one and all or the all-in-one:
Touch whatever in touching comes,
And,—brave beyond what may be saved
By what such touching has engraved,—
Never one instant's kissing shun.

Chain Chain Chain
[sonnet version]

Once upon a time, I had bruised slightly
My
Fing-
Erend in ty-
Ing
Unneedful knots too brutally.
The knots were sonnets, rhy-
Ming
Not gracefully,
Losing
Bout by
Bout despite my
Careful tying.
I had not thought writing
Was so much like fighting.
I stay-
Ed at it relentlessly
Tying tying tying
Every
Musing,
Bruising
blossom stylistically.
The daisy-
Chain was for no one particularly
(Or perhaps I am lying).
You know how things
Get tangly
When we practice firstly….

The leng-
Thening
String
Of words got too stringy
And self-involved in singing
That should have taken flight more singly
By
Whistling
Unconcernedly
And not too self-consciously.

Chain Chain Chain
[sonnet format]

Once upon a time, I had bruised slightly
My fingerend in tying unneedful knots
Too brutally. The knots were sonnets,
Rhyming not gracefully, losing bout by bout
Despite my careful tying. I had not
Thought writing was so much like fighting.
I stayed at it relentlessly tying tying tying
Every musing, bruising blossom stylistically.
The daisy-chain was for no one particularly
(Or perhaps I am lying). You know how things get tangly
When we practice firstly….The lengthening string
Of words got too stringy and self-involved in singing
That should have taken flight more singly by whistling
Unconcernedly and not too self-consciously.

Gifts Assembled

It was summer's atmosphere of doubt,
I said, made me uncertain what I was about;
Earth was warm and sure, I was not.
I made myself feel the closeness of the crypt.
To be by so much richness troubled
When wavery air gave me me myself doubled
In the very nothingness I breathed and stumbled
Was to curse a wealth of gifts assembled.
I did not have what I had wished;
Nothing did as I did insist.
Summer's ripeness came to a million *ifs*,
I had nothing but summer's million gifts.
All the lauded grace of giving was Time's;
All grace crowded close as living rhymes.

New Wilderness

Who incised this river here by writing hard
Forgot to leave with wetted alphabet
The charm of a cipher. The river rambles on,
Until caught up by the roots that shade
My going on in woods, although my coming here
Where river spells and spills into hard wood
Was open plain enough. And that's another kind
Of hard-to-see from too much looking:
Field and sky—at night, earth-dark and stars—
Flat each to each like paired mirrors with
Nothing caught between. So I'd crawled here
Morning long, the weather hugger-mugger nothing
And the fields off-rotation for bearing crops,
And, so, lively with wildflower wilderness'
Play-day maybe and beginning mischief
Of sorting out itself without the help of hands.
I thought, once, coming this way years back
On a similar sort of errandless errand,
I had caught, once, some evidence of pride
Running through the wild wood gone half-back
From cultivation to dark unplowed bewilderment.
I saw a line as straight as a forearm
Run a hundred yards between two equal
Tangles of trees—fair straight—the way
A stick will write out a line and raise a rim
In level leaf-mold chewed even by the time.
All this before a hidden storm the weather folk
Had laid odds against, and, so, I had dismissed.
And then a thinnest silver filter fell

And brought already damp woods as wet....
And I stood in the turn of atmosphere
As sunset brought a gold to all the air,
Infecting silver with light's last despair,
The way a fever brightens sickness to a shine
In eyes and cheeks, and brows grow dewed
With inner causes. I stood thus and wiped my face,
Interested to see such simple changefulness,
And not knowing why I displayed such interest,
Nor indeed why I had such interest to gift
To new wilderness come up since man had left.
But, slowly, as winter eaves will gather ice,
This line fallen before my feet, uncrossed,
Became a trough for an element not itself,
And rose cupping changeful water until dark,
And past dark, myself become as sodden
As my coat, my hands gone home to pockets
Like squirrels asleep in leaves,—until overfull
Of rain and moonlight. The line laid out
A silver bar, shining from end to end
Like some fresh first cuneiform stroke in clay;
You know how clarity can come on after storm,
No matter how minor the stirrings warned.
But I wondered, as I would. I wondered anyway.
What had taught the line to be, when clouds
Cleared away to re-present the moon to me?
What straightness lay here inherited?
Nothing came to drink of what had swollen,
A revelation strange as rain that'd left it
To puzzle one who seeks for things in things
And wants to know just what to tell himself,
Forgetting weather's made by being out in rain.

No Learning

There is no learning but to yearn and yearn,
And by wanting see what we think we are
(Composed of stuff from a farther star).—
Desire deep-in to recklessly burn;
Desire to assemble what all we are
By partial parts into one whole complete;
To work out the sum where integers meet
And write an answer without a scar,
Without a stitch where kissing incompletes
Tell-out by telltale the nightly labor
Used to unify our dawning wonder
That recklessly burns with day's own heat—
Until our in-dark echo cries for night,
Cool and apart, and all away from sight.

Down to Clouds

I'd thought life without Love no life at all,
And my life like a parachutist's fall
Had readied-up with a silken snarl
And without a parachutist's safety-pull.
I was dead-ready to meet the all-in-all;
I had all needed: gravity and a fool.
My heart never mistrusted God was cruel.

On my way down to clouds, through clouds to clods,
I thought how the silk weight on my belly pulled,
How silk and air stretched tight would make a shroud,
And what an act, inordinate and proud,
Living on would be—just as if allowed—
Before the cruel throne and crowded face of God,
My life one long fall as if dead and mourned.

By Shadow Known

I did not know how clouds could crowd
The weathered Earth by blowing round,
Or drop deep shadows by their light,
Too much lightness in sun's too much light.

'Til one day their dark put me dark—
Crowded me out by high-shadowed marks
From old communion with the sun;
Daily now my darkness comes.

I, who had been a burning cloud,
Now in noon-night perform my rounds.
Were I to shred their silver dark,
New light would blind by being stark.

Where

The wandering mind that wanders far and late
And wanders where from causal clouds the lightning
    breaks
And rivers thunder from blank riven air
Unhouseled by light. The mind is there.

Deep and deeplier, into the most low lightless grotto
The mind pursues its darkness unaware
Of how it does increase the dark it brings and bares
Where still the shark sleeps. The mind is there.

Out beyond this room, beyond the moon, beyond,
    beyond,
Behind the seeping dark that inhearses every darting star,
Beyond pale planets, back beyond where shooken
    concepts jar
And Time is dead. The mind is there.

Pastoral

A snake
Takes
The yard and
Garden,

Sways
As haze
Does;

Buzz
Of bees
In leaves
Insist

He list
And cease
His

Hiss.
They sing
Of Spring,
The beautiful,

Mutable
And mutual
Goal

Being
Is bringing

To yard and
Garden.

The snake
Takes
The song—

Gone
As one
Flash

Through slashing
Stale grass;

Returns
With burn
Sounds

Round
The garden
Fountain
Curl-

S asleep and full.

Walk in the Hush

The wind that tenses in the hollow
And re-weaves what grass I kick,
Goes over my length for pillow,
Weary of crags and dirt.

As I approach a higher place,
Barren and brown, the dust
Wind-blown into my onward face
Fingers my eyes and hurts.

I less and less the height approach
That further and further
Recedes; all that I now closer touch
Is the push of Other.

Why has wind come, why a stranger,
So close and harsh to me,
Who has no wish, no wish, to linger,
Held by what he cannot see.

When over the lapsing hilltop's crest
At last came sudden rest,—
I knew not who I was in the hush
When no gust pressed.

To What

Was it sudden ease, or the sudden cost,
That made us most feel we were not all lost,
That step and step had still some place to go,
That all the world wasn't but wilderment of snow?

For my part, I did not gauge the cost
(Or rounded figures down at worst or most).
I had no interest in what interest others took.
For my sole self my dual eyes do look.

I see the thing itself as it appears to be,
Visible from somewhere on vague reprieve;
Then I look where eyes look eyes-closed
And seem to hunt up a memory of shape at most

That rises toward some overwhelming feeling,
Rising, rising, as all else fades out failing—
Rising to what I always call my meaning.

Falsifying Fire

Our sullen retreat into the ever-there,
Our reliance on the invisible
Or recourse to given revelation,
Brightens my minute's thought to crucible
And pulls some lasting gold from my flame's care,
As if we knew our wishing and the wish were one.
What do we need of what seems infinite?
The partial glare of being here, just here,
Is enough of heaven to round our minute
And puts a light, however lone and bare
We cry for things more determinate,
Into all we seem to see and share.
I will not falsify my fire, but answer all and one:
No answer yet but becoming to become.

The Wild Hunt

A reindeer head and human breast
Prove hunger no mere beast
But a yearning, foreign fire all, great
To least, carry to life's living feast.
Tarry constellations stoop to whisper
In ears sharp as fine feathers on a shaft
What makes the unbrave whimper
And holds the brave man fast:

Undulant hills are too lonely
To have what raves in every heart—
Too unready to live solely
And nurture the dark feast that lasts.
Eat my starry heart, my body and my brain!
Nothing in Nature's self-renewing fast
Can feed what hungering thought may gain
From imagination's last and least.

With a light, clipped clop
Dunning into bright bell the dull rock,
The man with reindeer-headed top
Hunts the night, nor heeds the cock
Rawing dawn into existence,
The one near star whose agony stoops
To burn us hungry out of inward pense
With overwhelming wilderness for crop.

The Timid Leaper

Where an ArrowLine desert bus
Came exhausted to a standstill,
And made small swirls in the greater dust,
A long-eared hare on a hill
Listened to the engine's cooling clatter,
Saw pasty faces at grimy sills
Look out at what was the matter.

With fingerfine lips, from a cactus,
A stolen blossom became the hare
In the open purview of the bus,
One-sided with a crowd of stares.
Almost the timid leaper started,—
Taken by a kisser's shyness
To see so many lips half-parted.

Stilly as a waiting blossom does,
The hare attended the airy all
That sighed a quiet from the bus
(Attentive now as if stalled),
The arrow mastered enough to wait
For what the desert deemed or willed.
At unbidden wind, from dead-still
Into dead dust
                    the leaper leapt.

Interrupted Night

Two eyes followed me out of sleep and dream.
I could not dream what seeing things could mean.
I had deemed all an oblivion unabated,
A sordid compost of all I loved or hated.
Such was all, and all I knew of what
Dreaming sleep to wakeful reason brought.
But now these howling eyes unsocketed by pain,
That did not bear any look of ease or rest,
Stared green indelible thoughts into my brain
And came, unofficed officers, to my arrest.
The sheets I turned in, on me had turned,
As if in skins and grave-shrouds I had been wound—
My blinded body moved unmoored beyond my sight
And turned to return to dream in interrupted night.

No Effigy

A tree must burn to be.
When summer's fellow ardor
Comes, they sway up, the trees,
The way that flame and flame
Combine in a making game
When what they are is brought too near,
And are pulled apart by wind
Playfully alone again.
A large sweet-smelling cedar
Held itself all summer
As constant-shaped as flame,
With a slow, slow burning sound
Of leaves, and the settling tick
Of branch that knocks on branch.
Where the woods blaze thickest
There comes a woodsey *whoosh*
That undoes my breath;
All the leaves alloyed sun-molten.
The fall will show them golden.
What have trees but trees
To prove that inside fire might be?
Trees have no effigy to burn.

Assembling The Earth

To a Summer Hailstorm

I have been in existential hail
Since Noah first began to bail;
Hailstorm, shake me till my sadness goes;
Strike me till new blood flows.
Ravish mind with unfettered ice;
Let cold be all of your advice.
Thunder down and dent the car.
Remind us of winter with a faithful scar.
Strip skin to tatters with your kisses,
Only, hailstorm, do not miss us.
Tear the mailbox from off its stick;
Freeze the healthy and the sick;
Fill the chimney with cotton balls;
Catch the walker in a squall.
Rattle buckshot with heaven's force—
I am the target, you the source.
Disappear and vanish in a drought
To all but me, who keeps you caught
Closer than my second thought.
Magnificent blank in skies above me,
Stoop to whisper that you love me;

Like a naked cinder for your use
Seize me, hailstorm and muse.

Ordinary Things

There's a dark deep down in ordinary things
Resists our bringing them into view,
Or else in bringing them what light we bring,
As if to ask the question 'Who are you?'

I do not know what answer I would make
Being myself, and, so, invisible—
Although I know when I give or when I take,
Outfitting my days as I best am able.

There's a dark deep down in ordinary things
Resists us, the way a mirror pushes
Until we're left again with things as things,
Alone among our daylit doubts and guesses.

I am one keeps to himself, and although
I do, I do not keep the dark alone.

Wintering by the Atlantic
[Sonnet Version]

As snow and snow will in snowing meet,
What slid down danced into a wild sleet
And randomly clung, each to each,
Resisting ocean's disassembling touch
That undoes the individual who falls
And in that fall returns to ocean's all.
There was nothing there in what was of sky,
No help of light to help say why,
Only usurpation's snow-deadened hiss
That ended each self-formed singleness
Distilled from upper vagueness and the cold.
They did not fall because they had been told.
They fell because there was nothing else to do
But fall, and this the ocean knew.

In a Manger

It lay self-entangled, curled as ramshorns,
And pushed the belly into being mother
—Who, to be herself, had first to be Other,—
Which looked as if it didn't want being born.

Its sideways was more, and worse, than backwards.
It had to be sawn out to be itself a lamb,
Startle the clover and bleat "I am."
The bowie knife came handy without a word.

A tense scarlet torn sort of giving-in,
A clattering shape cauled on scattered straw,
Ungainly upright legs besides the ewe's,
Shook me wet and bellowed out of pain.

What had come too soon would need a mother's milk.
I pulled all night through wetness with raw silk.

The Paper Mill

I look into the portions of my thought, cold and dull.
Wheel in wheel unsettles the quiet mill asleep
And puts an uneasy harness on all I feel.
The river like a clock runs fast and deep.

Soon there will be paper, deep and white.
Wet slush from the chute, heaps of pulp and dust,
Driven by the living water to be a blank in sight.
A *haaing* gear gives my cheek a buss.

I pole a belt to the drive shaft, and all begins—
Horses in wheels turn, turn in their dreams;
Floorboards shake with purpose, dark and dim.
The razor nibs of the saw-wheel start a seam.

I weep, weep for sleep and do as I must.
I look into the cold dull portions of my thought.

A Blue Perhaps

The provident power of hurt and harm
The provenance of an eye ingathers,
(Its certain witness of a moment's charm
That lightly changes a life forever),
Bluely demonstrates in this morning glory
That measures us, our smallness and our fear,
With too blue an eye to ever bear
Until a touch of night shuts its story.
Then we dream, with a certain sort of blue rue,
And wonder in sleep's deep wanderment
If the sun will show us what to do
Or if dreaming can tell us what we meant.
An eye perhaps has followed us all day through,
But we do not know the eye's intent.

Water-Break

Having grown long words in fieldgrass daylong,
I stepped into a wooded brook to dip
Ink-worded hands into the snickering quips
Offered up by the silverquick stream;
I wondered just what the water had meant to mean,
Whose loose stones insist the water into song.

Many times I had lost what footing I had felt,
Suddenly cried out, or laughed in despair,
By hard wet things beneath thrown over,
Raw agony raised to the eloquence of a welt;

And, with water in my mouth, I'd often remarked
The sincerer operations of the lark,
Spilling a slippery noise above taciturn rocks
That break bones and never forget.

Rooted Things

Three dark junipers shadow where time stood,
Representative of my brothers and
Myself, from earth and water grown to good
Plain wood on the township's public land.

Huddled under them by the neighboring pond
Fireworks cracked to color July the Fourth;
We then, as I now, beside the dawn-like mud
Stood every year we'd been on earth,

Three stranger brothers our divided folks
Reaped as seedlings from the brick adoption house
Into a home too shy and shamed for such a name.

Now torn away ourselves to spouses
And lives, from rooted things by time unyolked,
I stand between the trees without a name.

Wake

I wake in dark. The air itself seems stained.
The dark appears a darkness self-sustained
By whatever of darkness must remain
Even at whitest noon. But this is not noon.
This is the dark without a shadow, without a moon;
A dark that won't stay shut in rooms;
One that follows even the ripest mood
And rots there, and will not give way to good.
This is the dark wolves build in woods
Who have no hands and whose teeth are sure.
This is the black that cancels the cure;
This the emptiest hour and the deepest hurt.
This lies behind eyes and bottoms every heart.
This it is that makes a faster beating start.

The Ant-Lion

His dusty body goes backwards to be dust.
On dust more frictionless than ice
A frantic slipping ant will make us wince
To see a crucible mind no more than claw;
A mind that harbors no dark thought to appall
But shapes his perpetual falling wall.
He does not jump for justice or to be just.

Summer's first rain-drop rolls in dust a world
Whose wet invites all wetness hints of growth
(Such a world may we recognize in drought).
Silent and dry, he emerges like a roar
And makes the molten tension burst,
And drowns himself with water, nothing more.
And a something unrepeatable is learned.

The Willow Bond

"Let's have a game of truth or dare," she said.
She snapped a longly hanging willow-wand.

We shared the field with no one but ourselves
And the willow that knew us from the play of years

That fountained alone and yellow in the field.
Winter's tears to April dew had yielded.

"The game is played by our both being blind
Until the willow tells true where true love abides."

A hint of mischief's smile filled my closing look.
She offered an antennae-end; I felt and took.

"A willow wand between two lovers' hands
Communicates the tension of love's bond."

The switch, whip-supple, wetly flailed,
Live as a shedding snake held head and tail.

I felt, where dew-bewildered life had broken off,
A sad pull; something, then, lent something soft

To our springtime game of gain and loss.
The wand had left a distance for us to cross

And reared between us a budded arch
Forever flowerless as frozen March.

"My question is: Will you love me all your life?"
"What you mean is: Will we be man and wife?"

I broke into a laughter I did not understand.
The willow sent it on to her own blind hand.

Perhaps this willow, being the ductile thing it is,
Adds a playful pulse to those it passes.

Something about the way the time compressed,
Or how the intercessor willow hissed,

Misgave me to give the game my heart;—
And that too went out along the drying bark.

What we are, I thought, we are by accident.
What happens makes us bend as we are bent.

I kept eyes open now, sure that hers were shut.
A glimmer or a tremor of I knew not what

Laid a furrow clear across her forehead,
As when question answers question as we'd feared

And not as we had hoped. The bond, the branch, snapped
Sudden as two children's hands can clap.

The Abandoned Tower

We drove almost to the mountain-top,
And had no wish leave it when we stopped;
No wish to leave the dew-enhanced, dew-christened air
That pleasured the lungs like a circus scare
When the sure trapeze for once escapes talced fingers
And the mind on sudden emptiness must linger
That had thought to catch a glittered body's twirl.
The thinness of the atmosphere made dull
The closing click of doors when we stood
A moment out of the car and out-of-doors.
Sunset took the higher half of woods
And the tin toy of the Ranger Tower
And showed us how a second Troy would burn.
We smiled to see just what we understood
As we stood together without a word,
Without the cluttered need to speak and yearn
That had made our road-trip *Cassandra and the King*.
The library had malformed our limbs
To wood, as much as books are wood, by sitting still
To read. We were over-ready to try a climb
Or try our no-words silence or try anything
To stretch out the long day of many knots
Our deep need to know had dearly bought.
The road swirled up away from feet at once
Round the mountain-top as round an ice-cream cone;
The road was rock and mist, the bones of clouds,
Red tatters gone redly under sky's west rim,
Like lashes of an agitated eye grown dim.
We watched small spots of dark swell and bud

And swarm up after us all the way until
At the last powerline we were caught
In a fatal undertow like a single thought.—
We walked on colder, with dark-adjusted eyes,
Still rounding toward the top. Things in nature
Cried out their alphabet of names, but none
Were ours, or reflected back any name we knew.
Our silence stretched between us like a clue.
Footsteps added footnotes one by one
Until we had left lower for higher ground for sure.
The tower sprang into the interrupted skies.
Spray paint through a lettered grid of spaces
Had tiered the artifact with conflicted texts.
We smiled once again to see nature vexed;
To touch where some derelict human trace is.
We grinned, too short of breath this time for speech;
We would have said a word or two this time,
For comfort's or for habit's sake, among pines
Where, in counterfeit of clouds, we saw our breaths
Touch. But we were wordless and rib-sore,
Out of perspective in a piney bowl
Rushing up around us like a garden wall
That aimed to keep in both flesh and soul
Within the clear-burned stone which grayly bore
The bolted tower that rose without a door.
We might as well have been inside a kettle
With the tower for a witch's ladle
For everything additional that we could see.
We scanned the structure for defects, but hurriedly.
What with the talus and its getting late
We knew we didn't have the time we had.
Still we gripped the rungs; they poured a cold
Beyond experience under our skins.

They were put here for a purpose, as a gate
Is put—to propose a boundary and suggest
A sort of going through. Of course, the jest
Is that the gate can't tell who's going out or in.
And we ourselves can't be sure of what we take
With us, in a purpose we call ours.
The sky began to stipple with young stars.
Each strut galvanized chilled hand to sweat,
So that we had to pull rolled sleeves over
Each rung, and get what grip that could make
To hoist ourselves a little more above.
Our collars had been thumbed up since we'd begun;
Our inch-thick sweaters had been left to hang
Like exhausted swimmers over library chairs.
Stars jarred and jumped—no, that was our eyes—
We took two deep sucks in to every one
That before our sojourn had satisfied.
What mist was in us at once would seize
Into ice spider-webs instantly as breath.
I hung halfway up a minute and heard
The charm of deadened church-bells in her tread,
Ringing on the upward steel as cold as death.
I looked around afloat in the tops of trees
Dizzy as masts and yardarms in a racing sea.
Night had come upon all things everywhere.
The trees put on their cassocks black and bare,
But refused to give a redemptive air.
Trees, gathered for prayers, stood devout.
The tower was all exposed angles and no lee.
She was where I couldn't quite make out—
Loudly made the platform on hands and knees.
Something of ice came down in shards.
A keening wind, whetted almost to urging,

Made me wonder darkly at the wooded ring;
The mountain leaned to windward
And snatched my shirt to tell me "Come and see..."
With a knowing note of something up a sleeve.
But this was more than would fit what I believe,
More sleeve and deeper than what I knew of me.
"You should see it up here, you really should.
Come up, Kerry, and hold me by the shoulders.
The world's as small and sharp as in a mirror.
If you shout down the mountain, you can hear
Echoes carry your own voice back, but clearer."
As if Earth were one to put our feelings to
Who never once told us what to do.

A Death in Woods

I kept as solitary as a wood alone
And often walked till all I knew dwindled to rumor
Talked from another country in a half-heard-of humor.
When death gave me up, I could keep the bones.

Today, having at last journeyed past myself,
I looked into a little wayside brook
Which, by caring nothing, all my nothing took.
I left a husk to worry a rocky shelf.

The Water-Mirror

One year all year I kept the pond for mirror,
And tasked water in place of one that broke
And so had run out of looking luck.
The pond re-made me foot to head,—and, nearer,

Showed my face as something like, no clearer.
Flat stones I scalped across what shone for song
Laughed at my distorted self the summer long.
Then one day in the polished lead of water

I saw what my broken mirror showed too often: fear
Of eyes in eyes, a black kept-back glance
Desperate for breakage like a last chance
To be itself something more than a moment's stare.

When autumn came, and I dared again look down,
A reluctant pond as rough as hands hid my face
For days, but not the sense of my disgrace.
Leaves above my pallid blur mocked me with a crown.

Winter's stintless nights full of wishes as a star
Drew ice across my mirror in a frozen sheet
Obscure and cold, and chilled a glance that
Knew me once, and I held back a shiver.

When my breath came back to breathing more at ease—
When pond had been blanched ice long enough—
I thought how roots go down, fathomless and tough
To stretch what stark water offers into trees.

The Timid Leaper

Then I looked again, with midnight thoughts,
At the rowans surrounding.—And then beyond all
    thought,
Far into the night, and past night to coming dawn.—
I looked into my mirror and hoped Spring again

Would wake it as full of fears as it had been.

Would Not Have

On an uneven roof comes midsummer's chore
To clear the flue that had all winter roared—
A core of darkness with a throat of fire
Soaring to a speech of sparks that suspires—
White-hot fleets into a world of frost,
A second set of constellations we may cross.

I cleaned with broom and water, a working witch
Fouled by the labor black as a sewer ditch,
Like pulling up a fountain by its roots
That has no cleaner wet than velvet soot;
Every swish and lunge bade me be a bear
Until an evening's scrub would wash me clear.

I heard a cry like a baby's squeak.
A bat. Something in me that could not speak,
But saw two eyes like spider's eyes to scare,
Gave the thought: I would not have him here.
Six million years had put him in his cave.
I sought to sweep him with the broom I waved.

We were too much strangers for the bat to fear
Untoward intentions in my coming near;
Our worlds were not close enough to make us foes;
(Hate's a thing of nearness as things go.)
I would not have him there, and thought to undo him
With a startlement of fire out of season.

So I built a fire to double summer,
Stood by the heat-wavered flue, heard it hum,

And waited like a cat for what would come.
In a laugh of wings, in a ring of fire,
What I saw fly out was neither foul nor fair
But a living creature of the living air.

(Face to face, my face was larger.)

I would not have….I knew I did not want
Such rapid flapping in my fireside thoughts.
When I look to flame, I demand to dream
Upon flame's own ever-changing theme;
Seeing how it prefigures in earnest night
The glare of summer, the stars' own light.

Because altered fire refused to move him,
I called him a black clot devoid of reason.
I used a poison. (I would not have him there.)
Congealing and winging in the summer air—
He fell out indefinite as a spill of inks
Dark enough to make me think.

A Wood to Sing Through

Our daily catbird in the parking lot,
Half-unknowing his danger where he stood,
Sang out eyes-shut atop a cinder block.

A blue abandoned Cougar, its purr removed,
(Haunted all last night by a pregnant stray
Hunkering into home in her birthing mood)

Had a dead crow's feathers like an exploded toy
Puffed from under a moveless wheel hoved tight,
Feeding what must come, at most, in a day.

Obliquely by her belly kept from being quite upright,
In cotton fog half-obscuring our shared world,
The mottled cat sat motionless on one stripe.

The catbird's territory song searched vacant grounds
That should have had a wood to sing through,
Not learned to be inured to all our sounds.

I wondered how I'd feel with the catbird shooed,
Mother-cat nursing uncurled by the curb,
Patched kittens purling dust just where he flew.

Silent in the silence man-made things disturb,
The cat, too quick for me to see, pounced once,—
And the catbird, leapt to asphalt eaves, sang on.

A Bronze Creeper

I had come too long down my own way now
To trouble with what signs dreamed appearing:
The simple-minded purpose of an arrow
An impertinence of trivial clarity
Pointed only to waves of vines that drowned it,
Getting more vine-entangled the more I walked—
Nature's green indifference a match to man's.
Mourning doves cooed the midday shadows soft.
I left all plans behind me and dropped intent
Back with those signs, and leaned my father's valise
Initialed in cursive gold against the last.
I would pick it up when I returned to reasons,
Sagging in voluptuous vines with a leather sigh.
Mourning doves cooed the gathering shadows soft
Under wavery arms of patchwork sycamores
Deep in the broken bounty of the wood
Where no sand-path of man or dog had stepped
To interrupt the easy gloom of leaves;
Indian Pipe and a fungus stump gave
A heavy odor the nose ignored.
The mockingbird with enviable ear
Talked to all his neighbors in their own voice,
As if by their sharing some outward wail
They shared some single mystery at source.
Half a sycamore had blown down dry
Like a thrown blade-switch in an electric storm;
Vines evinced no interest in its half-dead form,
But rode the living half half-way high.
There were whirlpools of vines in those woods,

Shunted hard aside all the time I walked them.
A bronze creeper takes its own time in ascent,
Using a tree's own strength against it,
Snake-slow up to the tree's own lofty end,
Like cloud gone everywhere or like climbing fire;
But more I think like fire than cloud
Or perhaps a fiery cloud come down
To threaten all that grew up from ground.
The wires that fuse back from its leaves
Tighten years against the tree-spine in a grip
To shadow-out leaves that block the creeper's light.
A grip once light as feathers, lighter.—
Yet shows the trick of closing tighter,
Hand over hand, or leaf over leaf
More properly, it makes its imagined height
Match the trunk's achievement grown up right.
They share a center that discernment sees.
But the outline, like a helix spun, begins
To burr and blur like an old old man
Who can't hold even his own old name in mind,
Until all the limbs lay overtaken
By a wilder interposing dark of green
That turns dry birdsnests out to ground
Or catches in an interlace of palms
Small-nippled nuts before the autumn-fall
Drops them to the danger of maturing.
How many years had I grown outbound to here?
I hear my own father laugh and shake his head
At nothing I had thought, or at something
So far back it was plain invisible to me.
Well, now perhaps I can sense the why:
We had been let drop to grow, for reasons not
Our own—chance, or even evil, occurrence

With nothing of our own doing in it.
We're left with nothing else to do but grow;
What better purpose has a laugh than sensing that?
Among a friendly roundelay of fieldgrass,
A sycamore has its life-plan laid out
From the first frond of its setting forth,
Unaware of how its reeled-in corkscrew
Waits to over-awe and overshadow all.
The grasses murmur nothing all day but sun.
Nor does the sycamore seem to posit
How its holding out beneath that summer sun
Provides just the slip of shade the creeper
In all its years of greenly slithering
Has learned to need. Once I came upon a giant
Sycamore sequestered in a neck of wood
Crowded as town, so hazed-over with bronze
Filaments root to crown, it seemed on fire—
The triumphal creeper self-inwound above
Even the crown of the vine-engulfed tree.
All the trees surrounding were backed away
As their live skirts might catch—but the effect
Was only the halo-emptiness of life
The dead tree had claimed in adoration of sun,
The slow outward longing of love's eternal
Intertwine of warmness and warmed being.
Here was a love affair too cruel to countenance
One side all terribly requited *want*,
The other too reserved to ever push,
And that was another story out of life.
I knew down in that those who would not stand
Oftimes retained the power of hands
And, seeming weak as lace, still could strangle.
This courtship would have no day in court;

A long struggle, and a single end.—
The corpse had a solemness, I'll give it that,
The way a bonfire dies down to ashes
And obedience. But it had no dignity,
Nothing of itself amid the choke and flame.
Bole and limbs still held themselves, riddled through
With spiny roots that cared nothing but to use.
A squirrel confused the leaves for a desperate hour
And then chewed clear. The creeper had no use
For birds, lightest true climbers of the wood,
And to their coming down proffered a net.
The creeper was everywhere and was everything.
We do not know our purpose, but onward creep
As a mood may creep day to day on fire
Behind our walls, knowing nothing but to creep.
These flamy bronzes too, were too desperate
Of their own old man's hairy grip and perch
To hazard seed beyond their flame in flowering;
What flowers came of that flame showed too poor
And too few to drop the match-head seeds.
New life must only smolder here this season,
However wary the trees of renewing smokes,
Thrown scarves to scar and catch the throat,
And envelope a head made blind to its own good.
The creeper, for all its bronze-fire threat,
Had no enemy but itself,—heh,—
And spent its life in extending tendrils
Of itself, all green willfulness and dare
Hurling its shapeless metaphor outbound
To some self-supporting taproot, to be
That tree, that life, if but for a time—
Stretching and warping its bare being
To another's bones, the way any son

Inherits his father's laugh, and in time
Has his humor, right down to the last laugh.

Aims

Bullets 'oft gang awry'
When we squint with lying eye
At the target we had thought
To level with a shot;
Somewhere along the barrel
Our curving expectation falls
And what is becomes a part
Of what we hope to shoot,
Or perhaps an intervening wind
Has changed beginning and the end.
The future always lies
Somewhere in the 'is,'
Or so the marksman's maxim goes
Hunkered in a bush of rose.
The future always lies
Somewhere in the 'is'
Our eyes are scouting now;
Hope and here intermix somehow,
Nor get pulled apart
Unless our killing art
Delivers to the shaping thought
The dead end we had sought.

The philosopher with his carcass
Dispenses with his guesses
—What would be now is,
And this is happiness.
Nor does he as he eats inquire
"What *if* I had not fired...."

Or if a speck of dust had interposed
Between his sightline and his nose.
All the dedication of his thought
Goes to digestion of what he's brought
From the wild field, as able,
To his domesticated table.
Not until quick hunger comes again
Will his thoughts curve and turn
To all the 'Ifs' of chance
That can cancel out his choice
And send aim or word awry
In the hunted day.

Existentialist Dilemma

The dilemma of doing's to 'have done,'
And by choosing from Many be left with One.
Addition's chief mischief is dubbed a sum;

The unwary mistake it for a total solution.
The wise contend that all is confusion,
Or at best a formal intuition.

To act presumes belief, or so I'm told,
And am pointed onward, backward, or upward to God,
(And reminded not to mind the length of the odds).

The less done the better is my subtractive reaction.
I'm not quite afraid to feel quite forsaken,
(Except that, of course, I might be mistaken).

One thought is left me, with which I'd begun:
"The dilemma of doing's to 'have done.'"

Good and its Opposite

There's a rhyme at the joint point of knowing.
There's a place, a way of saying, that clearly makes
"Good" and it opposite resonate, and even ring
The way a glass cries out when struck—

Sharing its invisible essence like a singer.
Glasses, brim to abyss, display a range
Of interchanging tones to the ringer
Who bangs the magnanimous Strange.

Does a sip sip the Good, or a sip sip the Bad?
Either way the song sways, half-empty, half-full.
The opposite of Good's not Bad, but
Odd, whose disobedient music's beautiful.

What words can we sing, for the Good, for the Odd,
That will make them ring out, spoon-struck, like God?

The Mental Garden

A rambling meadow scenery
Rank with irrigated greenery,
Showed a semi-sawed-off double dozen
Of saplings stretched since Spring, some
Waist-high to heaven, that autumn's
Clear-cut mowing would take care of
(Not much of disordered growth
Survives the park's enforced swath).

Nature's mistakes seed a scene
With a richer oddness than she means.
Plants that harbour high ambitions
Need time and shade for such positions.
Ignore me long enough, and I might
Just get to be something; kids grow at night.
Adults enlarge by thinking through
(So I've heard said, and think it true).

A modest eraser can undo
A millennium's gain by rubbing through.
I bite my new ones down to wood
And trust to cross-outs, understood
Arrows, and wild whole-page insertions.
Erasure's just too much exertion
And never pays for the lost word
That down the line might have proved good.

Human education is a crop
Best harvested without a lop.
Shapely shape the upward trees

By what mind kens, and heart perceives.
The grandest but add leaf to leaf
To make their roundness right—
Just so the round of human life
Requires a necessary height.

Definitely

In the right angle of a fence
Definitions first commence
To lock us into making sense.
By running round and round a thing
With a tape measure for a string
We hobble it to give *us* wings.

Its only from our having tried
To live without a *why* inside,
Or, like a mystic pray tongue-tied,
That we have ever given thought
To holding in what we have got
To see what we've done without.

Introrse Proportions

A clouded day in a warm week
Is little, in a whole month a week
Of rain, sans weekends, is OK;
A covered month of storm and soak
Is welcome in a year of weather
That puts sunburns and hurricanes together.

So when an inner barometer
Flails
      from hails and rain
            to shine and sweeter
And darkly back again
To damnably, darkly fail…whatever.

Roundabout

I had stopped myself at noon, amused
On an abandoned track that moved
Through a wood no longer used,
Through waste acres of a watershed
Cloven by a regular runoff where
Clarity was wildered by wild briars.
Until a hidden water's hissing
Showed that something else was missing,
One never would have wondered
That anything there had harkened
At the juncture where briars darkened
As if by deepness of the angle
At the midmost of their tangle.
Something moved beneath the plane
Where the interrupted track regains
The far oasis of the wood,
Something going crossways where I stood,
Crossways to my onward motion.
I stood without a blessed notion.
At the very precipice I paused,
And waited to see if what had caused
Me to arrive there once
Would cause me to hurry further on.
I listened to what I could not see,
Water in the dirt continuously
Spattering against such hazards
As its pattering traversed.
I spied the farther side, which seemed
Indifferently like where I was indeed,

A wood moving on to wood,
A leafy dark neither bad nor good.

A tree, once proud upon its ridge,
Lay translated into a bridge
At my left, and the track repeated
Its pattern as it retreated
Past the tree's, an oak's, fallen crown
Stripped to wires on the farther ground.
I put my foot, and it seemed
To hold upon a mossy cloud
With just a warning creak or two
That subsided like morning dew.
Another step, another crack
And I was airbourne along my track,
And the whispered waters loudened
To an almost-roar unshrouded.
This was something, then, a place
Unusual in the closed-in space
That gives woods a closet feel
Of uncomfort, of bodies real
But mentally disposed of,
The way we take our clothes off
And refuse to see them wrinkle
Any longer as real people.

Had the slope been undermined,
Had the tree been dealt an ill-timed
Blow by lightning an age before
My feet had brought me to this shore?
Whatever the history, I took
A naturalist's close firsthand look
At the detail that feeds the mind
When mind's to thinking first inclined

And all the world's a wonder
As perpetual as thunder.
There's an art, a large art, of course,
Comprehended in just looking close.
The moss had browned to gold, it seemed
Unfed by any mist or stream
Despite the pounding of the sound
That made a pulsing all around
Centered in my ears. Still firm,—
So then, just a dry summer's harm,
No more, curable by summer storm
Soaking live roots back to greenness,
The dieback of a season's meanness.
An ant with an aphid hat hurried by
Anxious of her fresh supply.
Another step, another, and hushed
Came the crumble where foot had crushed
The intradose of a termite arch
(Found more often in a fallen larch);
A colony of teeth in such bone-hard wood!
Whether bored, or because they could,
I could not know, and understood
That even in a thing so small
I myself could not measure all
By limits of my comprehension.
But now, done with desecration,
(Or, more optimistically,
Aeration of the tree)
They left to found another nation
With colonists from this way-station
Who pack up their idea of home
And take it with them where they roam.
And now the whole tree was hollow,

And houseless hoot owls inward followed.
Also into this interesting
Emptiness, came bees without a sting,
Carpenter bees who hustled and tore
Termite tunnels to a larger bore
For their solitary parlors
Conveniently near both briars
And water. Who'd've thought there'd be
So much of life in so dead a tree?

I had gone down upon my knees
In my investigation, pleased
To spend my day in something other
Than myself. I wondered whether,
As I stood again on what stood
No more, if I should include
What was father on out there
Now I had come thus far to stare;
My thoughts surrounded me like fog
In the middle of the ruined log,
As unsteady of my footing there
As unsure of my going....Where?
I peered a step just past my place
And conjectured farther on a pace;
The path behind was twice the gauge
As the dwindled path on the next stage.
It seemed that most upon this track
Had come this far to double back.
Well, I never have had more regard
For that stepper Kiekegaard
Than for my other walkers in the wood,
Intending to walk on as they should,
Instead walking only as they do.

I kicked a little nothing from my shoe
And made my balance come and go,
Unsteady and unstable how to go,
Uncertain and unsure how to know,
Kicked a something from my other shoe,
And in the end continued onward, too,
As few had chosen here to do,
As all who are not only bones may do.

To keep unlost, as doubt to doubt
You wander roundabout your route,
Simply do not doubt your doubt.

Grave Spaces

The town blind behind, blind woods ahead,
And a whitened graveyard here.
I stood alone with my luminous dread
In the dying of the year.

From the midnight hill I'd seen below
Huddled graves, yet each alone.
And here and there in the hollow, low,
A dent in snow without a stone.

Poplars dropped odd shadows, the moon
Dropped a mood. Whatever talk may tell
In me had talked-out too soon.
I brushed a small glow from where it fell.

The stony concentration of a face
Shone angel no longer—here the snow
Wears his worn-out years of grace
To the blankness of his soul.

His name's gone out like shopfront lights,
His verse survives by guesses.
What had brought me here was what night
Had done with my distress.

I walked out from being
And walked to having been;
Living was only seeing,
Death's just having seen.

The bell was black and the time that tolled
Was an absence in my heart.
Into those bleak letter-gaps, I had rolled
For all my part.

Wintering by the Atlantic

A midnight ocean and a stippled snow
Greyly perceived from a rail I know
Shared the grainy dark of here and nearer.
What water was above me seemed uncertainer.
What rolled in mist below rolled solider.

As snow and snow will in snowing meet,
What slid down danced into a wild sleet
And randomly clung, each to each,
Resisting ocean's disassembling touch
That undoes the individual who falls
And in that fall returns to ocean's all.
I could not tell just what my seeing meant
Nor how long soundless darkness had been lent;
There was nothing there in what was of sky,
No help of light to help say why,
Only usurpation's snow-deadened hiss
That ended each self-formed singleness
Distilled from upper vagueness and the cold.

They did not fall because they had been told.
They fell because there was nothing else to do
But fall, and this the ocean knew.

Late-Flowering Bush

Beyond the serious torches of several cypress trees,
The dusty chirrup chirrup of militant cicadas,
The noble solitude of a solid lonely oak
Clattering his leaves at the sun over a bleached field
That balanced his high growth by spreading out,
Desert-like and hot at noon, and all afternoon
Until the evening made them equal sharers
Of one shade, a blackness welled up from the root.
Beyond all this, beyond the blushing bluish grasses
And inner darkness of some evergreens out right,
I thought to see what seemed from the county road
A sweet hilarious patch of beech, tittering
Among more sober rowans, and walked on
Farther than I had thought at first to do.
A forest darkness hustled, a coat atop my coat.
And so I came upon a late-flowering bush
Hidden deeper in among more doubtful darks,
Taller and elder, more august and up high.
It was way out of season, much too too late,
Yet full of hopeful blossom regardless
Of the season's clock; it kept its time its own—
Before the long sharpness of the frost that tapered
In shadows till midday, it held its whites aloft.

The flowering bush was a thing itself, alone,
Clotted with milky flowers as large as fists
As if to claim a space among the harder barks,
As a child will feel more brave at midnight,
Startled from a nightmare, to smile in the dark,

Or as a father walks twice round and round
A house, for proof he really has a home.
The flowers asked for bees that would not come
To so shaded an interior, whose buzzed instincts
Could not guess to lead them there, too far
From the sugary buttercups and tigerlilies of the field;
The bees were busy with their honeys and their hives,
Too industrious to bother with this thing alone.
I wondered what had made the seed drop here
All those years ago when this bush first pipped.
Had some panicked thrush raced bewildered through the
     thick,
Or been carried dead by some hawk, and dropped?
How had the seed, which loved the sun, found
Filtered light to endure, in the coolness all about?
Had some tree burned out and a dormant seed
Been sprung, hot from its casing, into germination?
I'd known an odd old fellow who had not
Half begun to sing until he was half past eighty,
And his voice as awful as an old phonograph;
But still he sung, and mostly pleased himself of late,
And showed the lyric shavings of sharpened wit
To any too-curious; those words were his fists.

Above us all in the little clearing, the dull touch
Of a near cloud's inner-lighted immanence
Broadened into mystery over man and bush.
Something happened then, I did not know
How much until years afterward had stretched
My roots into some new dark flowing underneath.
But *then*, I did not know what I would become,
And, never having intended to be there once at all,
And having forgotten all about the patch of beech

That had first sent me off into the dark,
I shook my head at the flowering bush and took off.

A Winter Eden

A soft possible snow had descended
And let the moon climb down from the sky.
The world lay in whiteness without witness or end.
Snow lay on the tree-limbs like ladder-rungs rounded
And softened my cold need for why.

Not a blank footstep, not a note of sound
Intruded on the marvelous sight.
All creatures, all creation slept like the ground,
As though no other dark did our dark surround.
A winter Eden and a winter night.

And then I thought: It is *as if* some other than
The snow had snowed down or in,
Coldly immune to storm or reason.
Each hour I held that thought held only harm.
I searched the moon-snow transfigured farm.

The fallen night I found, I found no ease in.

Wet Weather Promise

Breathing close, I notice our airs
Have lately come as close to tears
As any injured feeling bears
A human made alone by fear.

Already this mist's been here three days,
Immune to our creator's rays;
Where it came from it did not say.
It has not gone again today.

Heaviness lingers on every bush,
Limned in weak whiteness near as touch;
All that moves, moves only to hush.
And, as I said, it makes my breathing close.

Once I was unsure of whether
Eyes and earth could share a weather,
Despite our eons so close together;
Now I know, I should feel it better.

Milk-Weed

A milkweed has it in it to become
Something, and challenges the field
With myriad pods above the other stalks,
And then there's the whiteness, all that whiteness,
Clumped and disparate with the wind slow,
A slow diaspora that struggles mostly
Into our reservoir just there, or plants its flag
In the same field that served as home.
There's that in us as well that never waits,
That wants out,—and gets out too,—past fields
It blows out onward always in the mind,
Same as the milkweed taken root and risen
To spurn its soil, and dies in seeding out its thought;
Just so, our light cares, light temptations
Lift out and abandon us, and we wish it so.
Some other valley's always more our sort,
Some other sunset igniting through the gorse.
Hand me that dead milkweed stem you've
Yanked up there—thanks. See how the lips
Have gone to beaks with vomiting dreams
All day long and under the August sun?
Here's one deep-in hasn't the heart for escape,
For leaving the only home its ever known;
No matter if that home is dead or soon to die,
Home is home. There's a reach in the design,
Wispy almost-nothing pulled to this seed
Soft as a moth, perfect for an escape
Once the pod's blown out, hardened to scrap—
Necessary for these feathers to move on

Into the endless. Rise after rise
Lies past this embankment of peaches, straight on
To the sea out somewhere, toward the Pacific perhaps
To judge by the wind. Never thought of it,
Although I suppose we all crawled from there,
But that's one home not hardened yet,
Not the sea, not yet, or if it had,
Something else has troubled it back to life.

Assembling the Earth

Look with me at what we call,
Substantial or ephemeral,
All of Earth, where we must end,
And all of sky's over-awning All:
Sense the sub-stratum and the theme
Dawning out of sincerer dream.
Note how dark must always end,
How Earth's quickened sharps of light
Coalesce by pixels until we see
Lightly lightninged twig-ends,
Dew-draped, shiver and invite
Greater light, or light's dark reverse
The odor of more crowded trees
Blends with the musk of night.
I sort my knowledge into verbs:
I did, I can, I do, I can't.
And other more *what-ifs* I list:
I shall, I wish, I shan't, I want.
And a thousand thousand others
Unvoiced, unheard.

All that puts a soul at ease
Enough to stammer and confess
The inconvenient, the gulped absurd,
Or to think a something mystic
Rather too simplistic,
Brings the daunting Earth to words,

And helps to carry, as you guess,
Our everything to is.

I kept a million themes beside my bed
In a rosewood box with a turtle,
With one working tin hinge beside
The turtle decaled spread-eagled;
I left the springed hinge untried,
And added blanks to the map
On the warm rosewood back
Of the rose-boned wooden turtle.
It was better, or so I deemed,
To live unknowing and to dream
Than know every meaning's means.
I kept the box beside me a thousand days,
An indian symbol of the Earth,
Unopened save as a question may
Discover unbidden worth,
The way a kiss becomes a question,
A new-burned feeling without borders,
A meeting, this meeting,—here,—
Solemnly together without a seam
In loving and in waking dream

A part or portion
Of the natural order,
Opening and answerless,
In a realness of air.

The Compass Rose

I ride the night-yard's rose bush like a saddle,
Burning to be nearer what shines afar,
And visit all the dreaming stars for marvel,
My rose and I still waking where we are.
All below is lost, I believe in what's above.
Unburied from sleep, I and my heart arose—
As full of feeling as empty of self, they say.
But knowing myself as I know my yard and rose,
I say, "Losing finds all again; there is a way."
Twenty years about both house and bush I've spent;
Twenty years dreaming to the rose-soft summit
Where the sun arises a rose and sets a rose.
Having gone round in love, I return to love;
I wake to see where my rose-dreaming goes.
My compass rose is cunning, her roots are deep.
I dream the dream I need when I dream of sleep.
The self is buried, and its roots are mossed.
Roots are what come of being lost.

The Sword Inside

A Dream Dislodged

Disorderly love falls on our lives
Like a dream in which we die
And cannot awake or dream otherwise
And only this dream is before our eyes

Ritual and rote and stigmatized
Inescapable and inordinately stylized
A sleepwalker's temptless step's imposed
And we see only the dream and are blind

Prolog of a Dog

This is an epic: shrunk, crabbed, and small,
Full of false-effects, self-pity, the merely personal,
A Don Juan who lambastes not the passing scene
But all that has-been Juan may be, or is, or has been.
Where more loving looks would gloss a blemish
The critic's eye inscribes a scar to cherish,
For every jot that takes away from fame, frame, or form
Bolts the sniping critic thus much more above the norm.

I spy inside to sight with telescopic sighs
The *whys* of my feelings' reasons:
Interloper on a landscape without seasons
—Why are such thoughts always such internal messes?
Insistent blots and bleeding
Awful as a Rorschach reading?
Or are summer ladies in their swaying dresses
The carnal cause of my distresses?
(Your guess is as good as I guess my guess is.)

Love's each word confirms what I suspect:
Disaster's the master, and we but the guests.
She sheds no sigh for any man's part,
Whether the nether gender or simply his heart.
On Time's high hill my glass house lies sheer,
White licked-together ice panes as thin as tears—
I'll throw nothing as improbable as rocks
But must content my anger by flinging dirty socks.

When confronted by the bare barbarity
Of a too-intimate, too-personal personal history

The titillating crowd contracts a gassy gasp
Into the actor's ruination of a yawn.
Put away the hugs, unclench the hearty clasp,
Poke about for the folded rulebook on Badminton
Or dewy martinis not cleared away at dawn,
Any of last season's or last night's amenable diversions,
No worse for the weather on the party lawn.

"But I have a tale to tell you!" he told the mirror
As a minor chord played in the castle dreary,
And like a lawyer at a settlement
Between heavenly disputants temporarily hellbent
He unpacked his tale like a holy relic.
He tried, when talking, talking about his happenstance
To concentrate Pure Mind from nominal Space.
Somehow somewhere something means something
As we fill with ephemeral words our eternal dumbness.

And ever the bleak bitterness of Love is present,
Awkward to forget, awkwarder to remember,
A golden goose whose taste has turned to pheasant:
Sour to eat, but the killing's pleasant.
Leaning with a highpower scope on my pickup's fender,
I forget at once who was the first offender.
A kiss is just a kiss, for all our wishing
And love is just another way for brains to say "gone
    fishing."
And yet what hopes are harbored in a sigh
To which all the pall of History can't manage to give the
    lie?
And somehow behind Love's final curtain
The essential something-nothing of ourselves is lurking.

To say that these things are only so,
That, in the course of life, such heinousness is usual
Is to dodge the lodging dart that conscience pricks
And with our green tequilas reel
About the empty garden like a crypt.
It doesn't make much difference
If you're in the Congo, Buenos Aries, or France
Time can add no savor but regret
To what the hand has done, or the heart inflicts.

Yet I may say, like the newscaster at six "Once
Upon a time, in a galaxy far, far away
I loved." Such a rare occurrence
Can't be measured by existential stirrings and segues:
It's the internal turnings of that monster Fate
That makes our mousing loves or hatreds great.
Is my mauve eagle of presidential pinion,
Or am I but a seraph's wingman?
Public puffs and public scrapes
Suck divinest wines back to earthy grapes.

The Sword Inside

A purposeless scrub plain laid before the sight,
Inarticulate, has nothing to offer;
Neutral evolution's meaning is neuter
Until interpretive man stands near.

Cool swaths and charts of haughty stars
Whirling infinite on a pin
To rampaging wolf and twittering lark
Revolve innocent of sin.

But one constellation-loaded look or angst-angelic glance
Cast up by blameful man
Can trace God's wrath in each twinkling coordinate
As plainly as a plan.

Until the intuitive outcast on the monotone plain
Divided the iterative day
Into the arrowy horror of arbitrative time,
Inventing vatic history,

God's mercy and His blood could not from the dust
Gather us to his breast;
Bhudda in his monk-smock howled the rice from his
    throat,
A proctor without a test.

Lacking sin's spectacle or anticipatory hope's
Human ability to fail
Life spins in a bituminous bubble of unbecome,
A whereless, whenless exile.

Narrow animal and expansive man both hunt world and
    sky;
Anxious and inscrutable they rave.
The one with tooth, paw and blind beak will kill,
The other with inner glaive.

The Ardor for Order

Once I was happy just
To flabbergast and gust
Over incestuous Thanatos and Eros,
My impulsive pair of heroes.

But now my erring mind
(Arranging, jury-rigging jigsaws night by night)
Surveys the surrounding social scene
In meditative fright.

The president imposes order,
The pope imposes hope;
Which one has the right to expedite
My sonnets with his ardor?

Every rhyme with *law and order*
Is enticingly narcotic,
But to impose them on the Zeitgeist
Is damnably neurotic.

The windbag of a fascist
Hoots and emotes in Life's emporium,
His whistlework's that of the serious artist,
Envowelling society's consortium.

His graves are all so neatly done
They lie down in counted rows;
The bones obey coordinates;
Above, there blooms a rose.

I conceive a magic bag
That holds us all together,
Or perhaps simply the spurious
Convention of "the weather."

There's no God, or need be none
(Intrusive into our intimate "Scene A")
Who's got to plod, or descend
Deus ex machina.

Draw instead in dreamy eye or fable
Something constellationish
Shared with elbows tucked at table,
A grace passed round or handed down,

The substance of a wish.

Evening Argument

i. She

A slippery sense of mental decay
        sharpens the knives
        and the wits of the wives
In drawers long locked away.

The sunset casts a spurious look
        to calm the unmentionable ache
        in my unmentionable place
With a Hallmark sort of trick.

But the hidden hurt must out;
        the curse must make its choice,
        match inner and outer voice,
And let the quiet heart once shout.

ii. He

Why are you so quiet?
        What have I done?
Silence mounts the table
        urgent as a gun.

All night we've argued mazes
        and all night the night before:
We see ourselves in the window glazing
        dart glances at the door.

You'd glad be shut of me—
        I'll be quit of you, I swear—
And in the going horse of voice and voice
        we bed each other on a dare.

My Beloved Enemy

My beloved Enemy
Confronts my chaos to define
My anger out of emptiness,
A solid hatred from rash wish.

My beloved Enemy
For my arch-arranging eye
Designs an aching target
That I must miss or hit;

Gives to my wide-range stagger
A more local, focal goal,
A sharpness to each dagger
Unfolded from the soul.

My beloved Enemy
Incinerates Laws like xmas-trees
And from a dwarfish, brutal bush
Grows adored as Truth.

Without my beloved Enemy
—Alone, or made by mirrors three—
No matter how I writhe and twist
My very self would not exist.

My beloved Enemy
Radiant with joy and energy
Looks out from my own interior,
Puts on my scowls and powers.

The Timid Leaper

My beloved Enemy
Alight with hate and ecstasy
—Fevered cheek to cheek we dance
Heedless of our circumstance.

Now my beloved Enemy
Made naked by wind and time
Arrives with a stricter chill:
My Enemy I must kill.

My beloved Enemy
Must learn now how to die,
And my beloved Enemy
In blood before me lies.

Burning the Vail

Let Love's lukewarm body lie
Drained of every lover's sigh;
Put up the crepe, pull down the bunting,
Pack in boxes the matrimonial trumpets.

Rescind the secret thought, and cancel hope.
Let marriage feasts go up in smoke;
Let the lover, loved, display
Independence to the end of days.

Heaven's research into love's prayers
Recommends ascetic despair;
Despite longstanding and accustomed use,
A gander's not as good as goose.

When the mirror spots in morning's face
No room for absolution or for grace,
Every constellation seems
Evidence of God's complicity.

To exercise the lover's part
Seems the only answer to retreating hearts:
Mechanics of hydraulic hand
Give no ease to loves lorn gland.

Modern convenience should make us fit
To enjoy the air-conditioning, and forget;
Yet still in every neighbor's bush
Lurks the same distempered wish.

Every kiss but seems to mock
Those lips no kissing will unlock;
Snipers crouch on every roof
To put an end to lovers' truth.

Ransack every inked-out line
For furtive hints of peace-of-mind,
Time the healer will not dispense
Relief when every breath is grief.

To be a ghost and blow unmade
Through drawn and yellowed windowshade....
What aught occurs, there is no stop
To distraught hearts or lovers' hopes.

What may mere continuance teach,
Stalwart survival of the leech?
Let pain cease, and let cease pride
When love's soft cause has died inside.

Intellectual despair
Indulges 'The Unrepaired',
While *Hymanaeus Io* wont console
Particulate memory,

> the ripsawed soul.

A Double in the Dark

Ideal and disposable, the idea of you
Rustles beyond my moony shoulder,
Amorous shadow of fictive love,
A dream demanded by the dove.
Shapeless bloods within me, grant
Dark nurture to this faithless plant;
Heart, beat on in dreamland to create,
Where a pink and rumpled pillow lies,
Nerves that throb in sympathy;
Create, heart, until I in moonbeams see
A second dreamer dreaming cordially.

New eyes open, asleep yet silvery.

Confessional moonlight's idyll
Which previously had bridled
In dry daylight's talk and squawk
Now lets our human arms console
Each other till the feeling's whole.
Let rosy midnight flicker on
Neon until the ending dawn;
Together in our sparkless darkness,
Exchanging jokes and mental missives,
Our only soft defense against
Outer Nature's rage: *This is not this*
Is wishing, wishing, wishing
Against compelling consciousness.
And our breaths' most secret heats,
Sirocco on rose-darkened sheets,
Whisper the stories of our souls

Where conceptual contrapuntal kiss
And simpler carnal lips may meet.

A new moon glimmers in the room.

By careful compact with the night,
Tangled breaths and traded hands
And tangoed bodies no longer stand
But lie as loving strangers might
Acquainted with mysteries of delight.
Side by side let us abide
Before that darling blonde, the dawn
Explodes and leaves in shards
The love we worked on *oh so hard*—
Let us have a meeting without an edge,
Nor wrestle with our conscience once
But play pillow-talk, be each a dunce,
Two drowsy loves, pale and veined,
A pair of frangible spirits' vessels
Laughing out the candles.

A new day glitters at the ledge

Unawares

I lived unaware for a time
(I have to admit it)
Unconscious in a casual castle
Sipping livid Glenlivit;
I was deaf to the daily curses
Of incontinent scullery maids,
And recognized not the stable boys'
Disingenuous praise.

As lazy time lolled on
From here and now to gone
A private contentedness
And not extant catastrophe was
What I secretly counted on.

And all that time, you
Looked over the lifeboats
Tested and prepped the crew,
Gauging the drop-height
From the second story window
In case of fire or flight.

I was smoking cigarettes
In bed, getting girls up for a chat
While tanning in a deckchair,
Eyeing the hostess on the sly,
And all that.
But you had long before departed.
The hallway echoed with your passage

As dawn or noon or night invited
The memory of your visage.

You had left like a bell
That rings only in memory,
Or how a tale told in childhood
Retold is a story today.
The hearing ear is fooled
By a wrongful kindness of the mind
Whose generous assistance molds
Everything it finds.

You are silent, absent and afar
Indifferent and unreachable
As a collapsing star.
Quietly busy ostensibly
In an alternate universe
For your light still spills
Some length of years at ease
In at every sill.

Ships and compasses
Still rely on the light,
Having been forged in your presence
And wandering still in the night.
But one day your light, having left,
Will leave us of light bereft.

And yet you return, return
In all the days of my thought
As if there were no now and then
As if mercury cornered stayed caught.
And yet you return, return
Like an agile ellipsoid mobile
About your own center you turn

Presenting new angles the while,

Presenting new angles the while,
New facets and faces revealed,
But really always and beautifully centered.

Maybe I too am centered, I too,
But more orbitally arranged
Fixed on a spar of you
From your central largeness estranged
As when Earth to dawn has come
Halfblind in the sun.

Snowbound

A silent fibbing moonlight washes
Distorted shadows of the dissenting sun
Over each snow-molested branch and bush
Arranged outside with a congregation's grace
For the terminal minutes of our love-embrace
Happening behind an unrolled windowsash.
You had wanted to hurt me, and did.
Truth was my only tribulation.

Your hands hung, inert and underfed,
Along the sofa's arms, overstuffed and wan,
Resisting the reconciliation of my touch
—And you pulled away, besides, your face,
Quick and moonlike, from my near face
Hurrying forward in a rudimentary rush
That had so often sought the complexity of bed.
Truth was my only tribulation.

It was then, snowbound and alone, you had said
Words that made all things one
And useless, in the gelid December hush
Whose winds diminished to a sparse trace
In the outer emptiness I could not face,
Too full of the moon's pale refracted crush.
I don't know how all this roomy dark occurred.
Truth is my only tribulation.

Pavilion Fountain: After the Funeral (Nov. 25, 1963)

Winter's never here at the fountain
Whose waters' liveliness seems a warm
And open candor. Things are but things and do as they
    must:
As in the fountain's pallorous spangling forever
Heaviness and light contest.

Beyond the torus of its halo
The summery waters' motions endeavor,
With the tear-bright dignity of an eye in agony,
To show how lightly may a substance go
An afflatus of divinity.

All things to their opposite use
Tortured, as when this lithesome watercourse
Was narrowed from easy murmur into gladdened sound,
Reveal some laden tale of their earthly course
Returning to their source.

As when like tears to ground we streak
And the opened waters that accompany burial
Flow in broken speech, so the startled water, at its arc
Interpenetrate of scattered light, torridly tumbles
All rainbows to one stone bowl.

Something had sung up
From the dark watered words summoned to console
Bodied brightness; as when we ourselves, by a terrible pity
    pul-

Led vocal from the womb, tighten and squall
To give creation's own

Cry to the beautiful.

Sestina: A Whittler's Self-Portrait

Tired of the afternoon, too tired to rest,
a crooked dropping spider made herself my guest,
dispossessed of the wood over which she'd labored
wispily uniting the crooked scrap lengths of pine
by busy inner habit for a length of time.
Unwitting where she was, she knew no reason

to rest here out of season. No reason....
Though with no reason myself among the rest,
I dare endure my time as long as any guest;
ignorant of Sisyphus, she had no sense of labor,
tying and untying her crooked knots of pine.
Reason's only reason in the absurdity of time.

With sly and candid step, each time each time,
a spider will weight a grassblade for her reasons
until the toppling tip on earth must have its rest
where busy man himself is a busy guest
by dint of crooked reason and crooked labor.
Too tired to rest, wherever here is, I pine

for bed. Each crooked plank was chopped from pine;
I lie and contemplate the length of time
Granddad who'd taught me hewed his reasons,
laboring and loving busily that I might rest
somewhere on Earth an honored guest.
And here again the dropping spider took up her labors,

surprising me upon the crooked wood I labor.
I watched her threaded progress along the pine

desktop chopped from scraps of time
when Granddad himself had thought his reasons
for cutting and hewing had been laid to rest.
Busily I contemplate my busy guest.

Absurd, I think, how the length of time we're guests
Shrinks, and crook my wood portrait while she labors,
going awkwardly on against the lengths of pine
as if it were no labor to labor all her time.
If reasons she kept, she kept them her own reasons
as we carved the scraps of day to silent rest.

Tired in my crooked dreams of tired day's length of tired
*   time,*
I hear my angry Mentors demand and reason;
I labor, labor, labor on my portrait without rest.

Agape

It's wondrous easy some days to guess
What at last we are and what's happiness.
Yet these inscrutable questions duly observe
Both the face of the question and the hidden obverse.

What do we know but that knit intuition
Pearls the stitches of mere superstition
When sacred instinct's emergent pattern comes
Divulging phantoms of what we might become?

There's no simple time in which to simply be;
Time's a dark palimpsest of what we can see:
Squaring the past with our parochial acre of here,
Or inferring a fictional future from fanciful history.

Flip, stitch, or analysis: we guess as we must,
Surprise ourselves, and end as dust.

Borderline

A psyche's inscape's treacherous,
As alive with dangers as with bliss;
The purple outcrop of a mental rock
Cripples the supple Muse and mocks.

Caught between imagination and the dream
The mind's barriers dissolve at the seams;
The motivating carnivals of lurid emotions
Cycles us like actors thru smoky memories and scenes.

Here we're running, running on the borderline
Half-unaware of the tailored baggage we've brought,
Half-amnesiac about the burdens dropped,
Drunk on our own lucubrant blood like wine.

Blindfolded eyes foretell dark prophecies
When we cannot see that we cannot see.

On

Beyond the paper moon
    and past the plastic stars
Lurks a lump or troubled wisp
    of what we really are.

Behind the pantaloon, the canvas and the grease,
    beside the green stage door
Lingers a loveable stranger
    whose tenor urges us to "more."

Although the lights are out, are out
    and the set's gone burning down
Still we ache to traipse the stage
    and immortalize the clown.

The grave is but a keyhole
    and we ourselves the key
That into clay or on to flame
    abide Eternity.

At the Gate

Beyond the bland suspension of a moment
    (still and queer and empty)
We sip our tea and take our toast
    drained of life and envy.

A drunken angel at a harpsichord
    suspends upon a cigarette
Some tattooed prayer of the Lord,
    some blank mystery as yet.

An opal in a teardrop
    confers what grief would keep;
Purpure absolution drops
    in gutters at your feet.

Starlight in a candle
    reddens the intruding hand,
Restless on the icy mantle
    where Life makes no demands.

Lucid Interval

You are the thing I love, no lie.
You have given me despair.
I don't know how, I don't know why,
But my faith has come from there.

I key my verse on my hearse's side:
"All our knowing burns down to 'Why?'"
—Nor give a fuck about my verses' pride
That they may live, and I must die.

Come with me, Love

Come with me, love, beside the oaken bole
We'll watch the finch dance in the waterhole.
Old blind men get their comeuppance
Whenever a loving two become
What's commonly called a one;
Only unlovers sit on the fence.

Come with me, love, behind the hill
Where the geese hold court on the croquet field.
Look at the terrible virginity of the snow!
Whatever is the matter?
We'll get the geese to scatter;
Only the unmoved won't go where's to go.

Come with me, love, uncomb your cares,
Mother and father are no longer here.
Take this white ribbon, take it and tie
The wildness of your black hair,
The wrongness of your despair:
Only take my white crossed hands till I die.

Come with me, love, into the sun,
We'll dare what they daren't when we are one.
Let the old man's finch and the old man's goose
Run to ruin and devolve to havoc;
We'll burn the prison and break the locks
And like the moon in water let happiness loose.

Beached Lightning

Stars and sand assault the sight
chafeing what should charm—
cloudy, angry—
a spirit's irritants—
until the kiln
of God's great unmated hand
closes close and fuses them
opinionless as glass.

Writing at the Park

Square sunlight on a square green field
Shows in a polluted puddle a perfect sky reflected:
The ordered boskage of the public park blesses
All those whose disordered hearts it caresses.

Love, with her careless powers
Marks or marrs our unable hours
Until desertion's our proof of having been touched;
Although the matter is little, the feeling is much.

Crossing that out, I then passed
A dead house with nothing to recommend it,
Solitary and unstately on the grizzled grass
And thought again about my sonnet:

Love's a whitened house with thin ivy trim,
Red roofing tiles almost caved in;
Its got attic eyeots to let out the stale air
Ninety long years had inheld with stale cares.

Soon I topped a big crooked hill that tapered,
And unsteadily almost drunk with the magnificent view
Settled down sweating to my dark square of paper,
Carefully writing while the sky was askew:

Love, which soaks up all connotations,
A paranoid obsessive of boozy inflection
Will cringe at each hiss, puff at ovations,
And in light looks divine heavy temptations.

A garter snake having easefully transgressed
My naked left ankle, I stood as I Xed out the rest.
One quarter's still blank; I'll try one more time.
Perhaps my tongue-tied Amour is a mime?

Love, the anaconda banded to the brow
Compresses all meditations into raw howls,
Cancels all occupations, the well and the dour,
And contracts imaginative maybe into definite now.

All of the objects (the snakes, the sonnets)
Distributed like rhymes in this Lover's Park
Endure the warm unlacing of the afternoon yet
And stay in stricter order until after dark

When darkness grants us all all the dark wishes
No acquaintance of daylight would ever wish us.

The Difference Is Less

"The neon fire Prometheus stole
Shown here before us as natural
In a painted campfire fuelled by laurels
Says stealing is Art's only real school;
Mimesis flames from Nature's manual
An *ignis fatuus* that kills and fools."

Museum explanations and the afternoon
Presume the usual, the accustomed track,
Drag us down to pre-history and myth
And then obligingly back.

"Before us both chameleon and sloth
In the surrealist jungles of deceit
Follow genome's and artist's plotted path,
Blend inhabitant and habitat;
So what could ever differ then, in pith,
Between boar's snort and man's snit?"

Among the crowded halls and windows
Our tourguide of the Louvre
Explicates Christs, perennial widows, the dice,
Hung between anonymous thieves.

"Since birth we're honed
To art and to theft;
To deceive to survive alone
Is Nature's tricky gift;
To get what's been gathered
By others is thrift."

Art and Theft

If a thief gave you his friendship, would you
    take of it and feel it?
Would you sit inside his patterned house
    among strangers' memorabilia
And watch his tongue when he remarks
    on the lamp from Aunt Cecilia?

The truth has always suffered,
    and the thief has always lied.
By law or thief or money
    the truth is never paid.

Raphael's Madonna, blithe upon the wall
    officiates *at* snooker;
Surely those eyes, so sad, so full, so wise
    they'd spot emergent Christ
Among all the convergent lice, surely they
    forgive the hand that took her.

The priceless art and conversation
    conspire to do you good;
You thrill that every turn of social talk
    might have a twisted end.
He recalls your foibles lightly;
    lightly, he's your friend.

So take the offset printed coaster
    that is offered obliquely;
Let the politely proffered crumbcake

sit center on the doilies—
And in his tepid eyes behind his tea
see if *you* are *his*.

The truth has always suffered,
and the thief has always lied.
By law or thief or money
the truth is never paid.

By valentine's the command comes down
to pen two loving stanzas;
You lean and stare and calmly crib them
on a millionaire's cadenza:
"Love is that which gives and gives
and finds in *taking*, splendour."

Villanelle: Beware Chimeras

Pastiche of paradises once pursued, chimeras
Simmer and shimmy, love's dancer desires.
In an era of boredom they glare from the shelves.

Our wanting all wanting by wanting consumes.
Desire's substance is fire, and desire continues,
A pastiche of paradises once pursued, chimeras.

Miss Mississippi poses and pouts blue allure as
We lust, Romeo baboons who drool for new Julias.
In an era of boredom shes glare from the shelves.

Kisses in a cave-dark hole we willfully dive in,
Drowning and hoping for anxious love's prizes:
Pastiche of paradises once pursued, chimeras.

Don't walk to their whistle or wink at their mirrors:
What's seen there's not seen, merely seen as.
In an era of boredom they glare from the shelves.

Fadeless as marshlights, they hate the actual stars.
It's fine that they shine, but not where they lead us,
These pastiches of paradises once pursued, these
    chimeras.
In an era of boredom they glare from the shelves.

The Silent Woman

The silent woman in the church
On nerves and vitriol does her work.
Doilies of the crucifixion
From warm young hands spread benediction.

Beyond the garden, where interred
Repose parental elders of the herd,
A picket fence keeps neat within
A few old sinners gone to Hell again.

The silent woman in the church
Tho' fourteen summers have blown away
Hiked up her heavy velvet skirts
Fourteen summers ago today.

And love was in her dawning eyes
And a wild slow dance in her step....
She turned a measure from where the graveyard lay
Like a promise not yet kept.

One Million This Minute

You've aged me one million this minute, my dear.
For you were my time before time had begun,
Your approval my watchword, my moon and my sun.
My cartelidged bones, once supple, now snap when I
    shiver;
The boys on the block wear thick Santa beards,
The pup that I kissed whelps broken-hipped in my hands;
I see them grow agued, and myself grow unbrave,
Full of hard wisdom and friends in the grave.

The hourglass pours eons in my ancient eyes,
I, who first saw you and leapt like a panther!
Like fated black clockhands, together we dashed
(At midnight my rest is murdered quietly).
I, who was once as timeless as laughter
And lived in quartz crystal; that crystal is smashed.

Spreadings

Perhaps my middle-aged spread, love,
Is made of despair instead of

Potato chips and beer.
The refrigerator's cool porcelain leer

Sighs and hums in weighty solace
Nightlong, and leaves a light on in the palace

Stocked with richest foods, assembled desires
Anxious yet to stoke caloric fires

That youth kept warm
By muscle burn.

The Thing Itself

In any universal force
    or unifying vision
An emptiness of intent inhabits,
    a blank of indecision.
To try and grasp the whole of Man
    must blur individuation
And see all wide variation One,
    innocent of division.

Who can blame them for their blankness,
    or feel themselves assured
That they have flossed Reality
    from the asterisked Obscure?

Wherever truth lies
    it lies becalmed,
Unmoved in its sutures
    by winter storms or squalls.
We come into our knowing
    neither too early nor too late
But just in a moment's glowing
    and take what we may take.

If you don't, as I don't,
    know just what a thing is
Sit silent, or politely ask
    the thing itself its business.

The Events Themselves

Happily at home amidst a blizzardy haphazard of papers
   dawn steeps the window with visionary promise
      for the entire apartment complex.

I am barren as you are barren, in a world replete with objects
   indifferent to our crux; I am broken and unwise
      as you yourself are broken, and both unclear
         and nobody objects.

Its always a trifle embarrassing to be caught in the act, to be alive
   isn't it? Coping with jaundice and child-proof tops, waking
      out of the same problematical nightmare at five
         as if sleep were the body's occasion for jeering

at the brain, which imposes its ordinary articulate order
   fetishistically every day on the bombardment of senses
      selling us fictions while telling it all, reporting odors
         and heartthrobs with equal indifference.

God bless the gods, apathetic executives of the irrational
   who are powerless without our laughable bodies
      to cast even a third-rate thrill—
         er, and make of our unable lives
            their inarticulate movies.

Discursive stanzas look like they're hurrying
   to the nowhere-somewhere of a formal fountain's
      repetitive static whiteness.
         What is left to say, is there anything?

Let love be the last letter of the penultimate law
    righting us rigidly as a strapping father full of laughter
      when like every incertain curious infant thither
        we totter and yaw.

And yet, with all of that said (so much) and (conceivably)
    registered in heart and in head by habit
      each day is only a day at play....

A lesson in how dowdy light becomes slowly a whole room
    and the grateful green leather chair emerged
      awaits patiently by the window its daily burden
        like a remembered word

its definition. Its in this way that we have died already
    died and come to this life, two civil persons
      talking together sanely, quietly, long-windedly
        as an aqueduct hums.

The world is full of sane sunlight and responsible landscapes
    not too impossible for believable humans to accomplish
      their unremarkable heights or average depths
        and whose prayers resemble steps.

But first a brief sleep, first order of business, then work
(not too late)
    may commence: every man must darkly his own
      unconscious Olympus propitiate

as when a mountain, unexpectedly on the horizon alone
    rediscovers, without notice or noise
      its monumental poise.

The Hydra of Days

The idle angling
      of a watersnake—
loquacious and lungless
      through yellowing waters
faded, sulfuric
      of a hurried traveler's Chesapeake
—through *tums* of evolutionary
      time still saunters.

Politicians, as limericks tell,
      are of a swift and similar species;
unchanging agile evil vile
      a Nepalese prince with an Eton smile
considers the cost of suicide
      the price of becoming a democracy.

Pelestinian flags
      on fallen Faisel Husseini
drape the dark Dome of the Rock
      while he's more leisurly laid beneath it.
Mourners wail until their faces congeal
      to unfeatured unsculpted stone,
blunted as snakes' in a pit.

Chinese warships in a watery ring
      lazily braid to enclose
the pale clarity and newsworthy brattle
      of independently little Taiwan.
Would cobras or roses be roses or cobras
      if they could be persuaded to choose?

Another day, another hour goes
        cold-soldered to the chain.

State Street bagpipes and banners
        play old Joe Moakley to rest;
dead as he'd lived, paraded,
        by cries and high casuistry followed,
down to the crypt and the Beantown dirt
        he lies interred with the rest,
another day snaked to the flow.

"All change as they die,"
        is the evolutionist's cry,
"and all ways wander unlost
        toward the one wild Great Way.
Each creature encircled
        beneath the infinite 'Ifs' of the sky
is trapped in the hydra of days."

Memo for the Millennium

Muscular terror swipes at our skins
    with its professional ironblack hooks,
Peers in at every evening window,
    flashes out of every book.
Defined by what we fear, we each begin
    dawn within a mirror's hollow look.

Terror's all eagerness and action—
    a nightmare thing with wings;
An Anthony Hopkins' Hannibal, one
    horror that glares and preens,
Agitates all hearts like flippers, and thumps
    at the back of every scene.

Before this lonesome sojourn launched
    in Body's leaky boat,
Did we hesitate on the angled grass,
    touch toes beneath the moat?
Did we dream of all the dreams of wanting
That lifelong flock about us,
    circling and taunting?

But here we are, and that's the main thing,
    hugging ourselves in shopping malls,
Screeching at the top of the swing.
    Our lonely unaloneness should appall
But is itself a kind of lovely;
Or so I think the angels think,
    hovering abovely.

Origins & Ends

'Tis said our end is half-divine
And our days leave but a broken track
That moves, when it moves,
Neither here nor there,
But shuttles forth and back.

I heard our origins are in the sky
And we crawl in fallen estate,
That when we stand
And cry 'gainst God's plan
We moan more than half-way mad.

'Tis rumored in our veins
That sex is a wish ape-uncles had
In a forgotten forest glade
Evolutionary urge made glad
And figleaf now forbade.

I know my heart's an Argonaut
And sails on waves of pain
Toward adventure and to a land
Evolution and God forgot
But like a sleeping seed long has lain
In Imagination's open hand.

Off the Coast: the Castaway

Our interim swimmer
The flotsam of a dreamer
Will drift and shrug on whatever log
Drifts and shrugs along.

Among warm fantasies of existence
He'll pip himself a prince
Or surmise a wisp a whip
Coiling angrily at his hip,
His own dark, androgynous
Urges to nip and sharply shape
And torture into consciousness
Speech where a beast would gape.
Forgetting in the momentarily kind
Regard or design of a cumulus cloud
And friendly D vitamin sunshine
How a taut tiger might lie supine
Between the shadow and the visible
He considered that nature and nurture
Had made him of all things the richer.

The circumlocution of the clouds
Said nothing to him; of this he was proud.

He thought: to be awake but unaware,
To not be subject to thought's despair
Or consciousness' superstitious care
That inscribes the history of the tribe
Into every member's singular side
—A Rotary Club tattoo, the gestural

Cool of a Crip or Blood's hand signal
That had DNA for its original—
Is to give up or resign
Your part in the human sublime,
To abandon the spiral nadir
Of accomplishment's stair
To the deterioration of clumsy Time
Dirtying suavity's shine.

A barracuda acting as it was told
Skirled to the surface, garish and bold.

He thought thinking was almost all.
He thought that since the fall
From preconscious One
Into the active energy of Become
That History and all of her messes
Devolved to individual "bless yous,"
And the scale that shows this depth
Can be reeled off in a breath
By any mammal whose consciousness
Swims livelier than a fish.

From a wet and worsted pocket,
With an uncareful, watery shift,
He brought a palmed mouth organ out.

And he thought as he floated there
Between ecstasy and despair
Between the sweet green-glowing swells
Of his mild Cape Hatteras hell
That the shirring, Shelleyan lute
Could be plucked only to confute
The rare, the rightful argument
That evolution in the docks presents:

That obscurity obstinate and disguise
Are designed by chance to make us wise
And lift us by gimmicks to Eternity
On whose verities we may spy.
By the regularity of genital function
By the pageant of reproduction
We place opportune or Platonic kisses
On wicked lips or wicked wishes
And spurt our progeny toward Heaven's swoon,
And like the tiger we sleep at noon.

Darkness

Heavy, unforgivable dreams, despair,
Hard breathing, the omnipresent air,

Whistle beneath my brain a tribal tune
Uncaught by inner ear since Stonehenge rune.

Waking in a shuddered fever
Unconscious of pattern or the weather,

Ripped apart by an ambulance scream,
Torn to storm-cloud crepe in dreams,

The question presents itself undressed:
What's happening? Where's Death?

What's my cause, my case, my crux?
Horror stirred to eloquence

Returns the steady stare,
Blatant or beady, that I did not dare.

By failure of vision we unite
Where all the candles refuse to light

At the black bottom of a bowl or ditch
Where every nerveless hand fumbles for the switch.

A Lighter Ballast

To balance a friendship's difficult.
To give's difficult, to take's difficult,
Difficult to offer the enduring cure
To caustic inward hurt and to outward time
Where nothing's ever certain and less is sure.

One must always be willing to offer a sacrifice—
A clattering frag of the poor apportioned self let go,
Give the altar fire a fist of flour and rice
Thrown into the forward void of hope. An ego
Can be a convenient casualty at three.

A memory of wiped eyes deployed at four
Can settle noon's uneasy moment, and by jettisoning
    restore
A lighter ballast to trim ship and sail on.
A calm cool hand on a vomiting neck is displaced
By the necessary zero, placeholding what's gone.

Jaded jokes traded over a toke and a drink,
The topical hour tossed off in a walk
That helps a mellow pair of humans to think—
All can be branded and bundled and bade fair farewell:
Your cost of continuing's their going to Hell.

Lose it and be happy at the loss,
Pay it and be damned the cost.
Friendships no less than civil societies
Send out their draft notices to the soon-to-be-lost;
Death's the price to maintain us at our ease.

An accurate accounting is friendship's worst curse
For, accurately speaking, however equit-
Able in feeling, all friendships divide at
The punctual inequality of a hearse.
So joy as you may and addition be damned.

Don't look to friends for your conclusions
While you nod and hum at their confusions
(As maybe they will nod and hum at yours)
And in this charmed essential interchange
Do not dream to esteem yourself the worse

Because of angry antsy things either said or did
(What dark horrors brightly shown, what honors hid).
After the humiliation in the kitchen
A friend will still do as friendship always bids:
Exert persistent force for modest growth
        inexorably as lichen.

Constellations In December

Xavier Descends His Soap-Box

Every day there was a little less of himself,
A moon of diminishing hues,

Less and less, as he strode from the balustrade
To the roses, each night a different leaf fallen,

Each day a new ambivalence in the sun's assertions,
Proverbial gold in a stale world

Where the water tasted tinny and the tap spat
Erratic chuffs of water in an empty cup

And something or other had died a day earlier,
Had died and had its poor death recorded,

Less and less itself, or its wintery twin,
Pacing from the terrace to the garden.

Cloudy Apostrophe

Calmed lightnings in the evening sky
Shuttle, like warm humans, from sty to sty.

If ever there were an evening readiest
For comparisons, gilded in flashes, half real,

It is this evening, blotched by light,
Spumed with cloudy figures of our imagining.

And so the erratic discharges of our thoughts
Are themselves significant,

Indicative perhaps of the circuits that we make
Circling one disaster and another catastrophe,

Symptoms of a discord so profound,
Malevolent fragrances of black, pitted things,

That long-fruited hopes have withered, and everlasting
   airs
Crimp their silvery middles tiredly

And the brazen horizon awes us a little less
With its simmering magnificence

Dull a little, and a little cold even in summer,
Shunted to one side a little, and old and used.

Wormy lightnings, restore the discords of your colorings;
These are the makings of our end.

Remote Chiaroscuro Enters West Virginia

Is it a death of the self, or of the self's
One projection, fatal ray, deadliest beam

Unfolding from out of a stillness the self contains
Like scissors, or a dove's placid wings, abruptly flown

From brooded palms, this quiet that returns
To the stone house, empty and white

In a whiter air? Something deeply tired
Has taken the place of the cows,

Still morose, filling the entire structure
With placid breaths, but what is it?

Is there, in this fix of airs, an extinguishing anguish
That broods from the barn, the tired reds

Falling in the air under a Dutch hex
And a soggy roof buckled by the weather,

Something that ticks in the empty hayrick
Or yawns from the creosote timbers

Leaning together a little in the space left
By the solemn breathing of the cows?

Among the Shadows

The pines in their shadows are distinguishing themselves
Detached in a softly shaking emptiness

Separate from themselves and their riveting greens,
Voraciously vivid, beyond coughed words,

Beyond a last leaf stretched in a last silence
Like Hamlet at the vacant end of the meadow,

Dying in summer, breathing a last breath
In the final rye and grasses, seeing the trees loud sway

At the rim of the yellow field, shaken
Softly, softly, following a blue track through the pines.

Flatterers Among the Roses

Does the moon sail in its sumptuous heaven
Disfigured by pity,
Blindly tearful in an icy lair?

To walk in the moonlight, to trod
The verdant ambers, and to think of nothing,
What sort of matter for a poem is that?

Is it a matter of having nothing
In the mind, icy sequester
Of nothing, of nothingness layered in its own absence?

Or is it a matter, rather
Of nothingness icily conceived, icily meant?
It is a matter of sinister consequence.

To walk in the violet moonlight
Discussing the moon from which it flares
Disfiguring the roses

Is a kind of nothing, a suave
Hollowness that we may hold near
Or suspend between us as we walk.

O savage celestial, misty moon,
Snarling in your lair, speak,
If speak you must, in dismal syllables

Some more blatant human meaning.

Loquaciousness in Louisiana

Picaresque birds cry hi-yi-hi
From the lustered branch
Festooned with ants.

Crocodiles mustered in the bayou
Flutter melodious tails
Under oaks.

Captains of the stratosphere march high, march high
Stepping the squalid dews
Of gaudiest clouds.

When the marshal of the swamp cries hi-yi-hi
It is his essences' valence
Neatly strummed.

Aperitif in November

Standing a long time before the pond, in November
Standing and looking at nothing

Or looking and forgetting it is oneself that looks
One begins to think

That the sinewy residue at the bottom of the pond
And the pond, and one's consciousness of the pond

Moving over it like an enigmatic cloud
Are one, that the famous watery veils are no longer

Waiting to be torn, or that, torn already,
They have left only these sinewy shreds,

Gluey blacks thinly dispersed in the space
Between the self, astutely observing,

And the brown pane of water that lifts the clouds
And the bottom of the pond.

The Condition of the Furniture

When the house stands empty, the rooms disgorged
Of all the crumpled laundry daily life imposes

How conditional our maundering sorrows seem,
Another routine, like sleep and death,

Engaging our restless spirits
As soccer in Brazil, the overnight weather,

The uninhabited chair, weighted with fringes,
That stares in the leaning mirror morbidly

Or the dirty shovel that leans in the garage,
A little old and uselessly, by a mended fishnet.

The Mannikin Grown Large Again

One has lived long enough
Among rusted hills, and the solemn sunlight

Spinning its steel shadows out of itself
Over those hills, thickly gathered at the arbor

Where matted vines still move on the latticework,
Purple embrasures, seeming almost to speak

In a light that is constantly fading,
Shifting its emphasis, a sliding center

That creeps over partial hills,
Real where revealed, invisible elsewhere—

Full of hidden masses and interior kisses
The way a sliver of grass is an entire field of grass,

The way a man represents a man,
Without feeling, in the inhuman landscape.

A Capella, A Cape, Agape

Dun Madonna, caped and veiled
By modest night, the color of shale,
Unclench the spools
Of moroser weather
Tucked by fingers beneath your vermillion cap.

Unclench the spools
Of angrier rains and redder tornadoes
From your tense cap
While the violet moon's sisterly sap
Drips bip, and bip, and bap, bap, bap.

Her slender tongue
Unwrapped the whitest portions of the night.
In the hills, green winds prevail.

Solar Resignation

The sun, scintillating cadaver,
Refusing blue, or mauve, or sincerer purple

For the great step he was to make that day
Entirely out of himself and into the world

Where dull mauves congeal, purples espouse darkly,
And blues irresolutely go blank,

Unpacked his scalding instruments in the dark
Listening to the machinery of crickets, grown tired,

The imperceptible brrr
Of cold discomfort that enmeshed their foils

And, tired himself, threw the rude cash of light
In the moon's urinal.

The Native Muse of This Rock

The native muse of this rock
Wakes dumbly in the morning mist, and in the garden,

Attaches itself to a cockerel by thin tins
Of light from the bleakest planet;

Wakes, and stumbles about the house in a robe, having
     misplaced
Dawn's engines, the consciousness of a dawn

In the folded dark of sleep, last night
When, by the bedstand, it seemed a few syllables had
     made life cohere.

The native muse of this rock, dumbly awake,
Preens against an obliterating light.

The Butler of the Weather

The butler of the weather,
Essential lumin on a globe gone dark,
Parsed us out upon the table
With a certain ceremonious, filial delicacy.

What we were we were, without detail,
And so was he, tracing his investigations out
The way a dachshund traces the motivating fuel
Of furtive foxes darkly red.

Even so, rising to its perch
A bird of poignant recitations
Cries sky and sky and sky
In American barrenness.

Each thing in the evening tried to find
What sort of thing it was, and how it had arrived
In the evening of which it was somehow a part
As stars descended

Over Florida.

Variations on a Viol

The builder of cellos in solar weather
Extracts a suavity from knots, true trills
That mock the swilling catbird in his royal chair.
But from what seed increased the pilfered wood?
Farm boys and their milky maids grown old
Must, as hale timbers rudely weathered,
Must strain, and crack, and, in their scale, break
Remoter love's fiercest chord, dwindling
At length as even the grandest cock
Goes rolling, listlessly, on to noon.

II
Blue rabbis without hats are chasing still
What rabbis, bending at their lamps, construe
To be the bright perennial, in renewing hues
Emerging, out of so much ephemeral dust.
Hearers of thunder in their flamenco capes
Make much of its minor terrors and mimic hate;
Dividing time between one disaster
And another catastrophe, that kills,
They are like drowned rabbis beholding doom
In a stoven ship of their own imagining
While blazing fish peek about their bones.

Mud Slide in Vernal Weather

You can see the earth shake, no doubt,
Its myriad images
In your broken glass.
You can feel it, no doubt,
In your tenebrous nails.
Or in the nervous laughter that the sky
Shakes down.
Pointed voice, mixing blues and browns
In a vivid mash that riffles the eye,
These solids, and these,
Remain impenetrable.

O how I regret not having killed
The mouse in my childhood.

Enfold me, lucid muds,
I would go cloaked in earth the way a duck
Dons water.

Fluxes of Ephemera
for Amy

Disconsolate in the deepening weather
Of a miserable December,
Cincinnatus made a house of song
Pinching out the solar imperative
From other, more miraculous strains
That salted the winter air
And coated the simple ice on the porch.

Without aids in impossible weather,
Cincinnatus made a house of song
And took up, in primitive measure,
A primitive abode.

A Questioner of the Weather

Less and less sure, O soul, the rain
Repeats its residuum
Blanking church bells with its ultimate referent:
Itself, or some other final thing
That bears the buffets of ceaseless existence
Like a paper that rolls over in the wind
Or the wind that rolls the paper, which,
Startled itself, is full of paper sounds
The mud on the moon illumes.

The rain is rasping against the panes.
A dark, familiar change,
Elusive elysium, starts at the edges of the ear,
Chewed by flies in a forgetful sun,
Hollow as a father's falsest word
Before drunken dinner, sheds its drunkenness
On a few, familiar objects.

What word will ward these mute excursions?

A Mockumentary of the Sun

One bakes and waits in the roisterous sun
Tapping out universal time with a particular foot,
A principle shoe, worn leathers unable to reflect
The merest shard of all that solar crisis
Burning in the sky and in the apperceiving chest
Like boxed jewels winking out of showiest velvets.

One waits for the desert to be done with itself
For the holy sequoias to drop their arms,
One more martyr, torn down by storms,
Reduced by the sun to one skull of dreams
Throwing one more shadow away from the hill
Like a river that flows out of the mind at last.

This earth of cakes and sweet excrescences
Lets us eat the loam, lick saccharin sands
From our lips, taste smeared blazons of cotton candy,
Raspberry and chocolate, the florid saps
We bite from the tree, laden with glistering fruits
We ourselves have made, and ripened in each eye.

The Soft Assault

Unfamiliar Places

Atlanta, GA

Dearest J,

Unfamiliar places make me long for your familiar body. An ardent urgency I had not suspected distance could supply has brought your sugarpot to a sudden boil among the peach boughs.

Tonight, you spoke of "living in the now,"—and how I long to let my soul do so! My heart is a history of desiring—desiring so strongly that it crushes whatever comes to it (good or ill) until that thing becomes integral with itself. This is my meteoric bliss and patchwork, bastard and disastered composition.

And yet—how deeply and completely I long for thee! Dark vintage of my nights, coiled bedmate of my days—our hours toiling in the sheets or embroiled by our tongues, I long for them all again! The crown of the root of my cock has been too long unbruised by your cunning junctions.

The Gossamer Gauntlet

"You are a ruby encased in granite."—Rumi

Dear Quixotic Fox:

I know that you said my poem horrified you. In the poem, I was trying to give the classic abstraction of "Gender" a voluptuous body.

I also know that you are afraid of the verities we have already shared and which we can share again in any moment you want to pick up a phone and be in my ear and in my heart. It is your own fear that stops you, and nothing else.

Listening Hard,

Ruby Granite

Life's Too Short For Unsent Love Letters

J,

No. You should not see me. It's impossible that you should. For, you see, I love you. I love you like the open sky, endless and magnificent and empty. It's not reasonable. It has nothing to do with control or wise decision-making, and much to do with hurt and with joy—both equally. That cannot be for you. It's impossible that I should love you, that I should have these feelings and these wishes for one whose heart I do not know—who is a mountain in its mists, observable but unknowable. It is not possible that I should be able to ascend it; neither may I reside at its foot in peace—it's shadow has touched the shadow of my soul, and I am shaped by this glimmering darkness called life. Stay where your life is all yours and none of it is given away. That is best. Not this folly, this parade, this ignorance, this mystery. Abide and be well.

Gregg

Living Alone and Dying Alone

Mole,

Living alone and dying alone is something that all of my "artist" friends have had to come to terms with—and its the one fucking thing that kicks me in the ass all the time and that I steadfastly hate. It's the worst shit to me. But everyone with a point-of-view feels it.

A lordly friend of mine says its what gives him the courage to stay married (scary)—because he is SO alone. One friend has always put forth that point of view—utter alienation. Yet—what a crock! If I believed that, my good Mole, I would drink every day, souse my brain and sauce my heart with soul tunes and blues, buy velvet sheets, rape anything that walked, piss on the innocent, and beat on the sleeping.

What guides me is not what I "know" about ANYthing—but what I hope for everything. And, since my imagination CAN, literally, encompass the known and unknown universe—I've got a lot of responsibilities when it comes to making that imagined universe dream itself to truth.

Yrs. In Glory,

gregglory

Half animal and man

Half animal and man in my shambling frame
I ache toward the open doorway;
wounded and wronged in my make-believe flesh,
blazed and amazed by a million teardrop eyes,
my every ear alert to illumination
in the star-flying dark and flak daylight-
I hunch against the wind of forever come.

Banquet

Sick ink
vomited belly up on the throw rug
as if I had forgiven it,

the swallowed ball
of my poisonous poem, a loaded ode
to limitlessness and light—

What trash!
as if the sky—vapid and superior in its imperial blues
didn't know how to bite!

Mistakes, mistakes!
The pen's a miracle of mayhem, wild slips
of a wrist once slitted;

the bleeding, careering nib,
a molt of details in the schizophrenic flow:
my mangy life,

my frozen embryo
carelessly cast from the shelf, unlidded
and palely little.

The cornflower fists
ache to begin, the watery lungs
two skinned, amniotic fish.

A bonfire, a bonfire!
Something huge and ruinous with real red in it!
That's what goes, what really goes

with this stone decor,
this face hung in a mirror slashed to tears.
Heat, heat

anything to exhaust
this caustic blank in my being, torn calendar—
Journals, drawn loves, alien lines

poems mouthed from poems
—dead-weight papers pushed to a death heap!
a Jew harvest at Dachau—

Perfect things
as final as a corpse,
ashes to ashes.

The matchsticks itch
to finish it.
Irritable Rubicon

of lava, language vulcanized on language,
I cross you languidly.
I am nearly asleep

in the oxygenless air. I am tired, tired,
tired of curses, tired of cures
tired of the alphabet.

The wall, infinite sheet,
turns intense as an oven, the nails
must be melting…

And here I stand
awash and exhausted, perfumed in the rolls
of corpse-smoke,

words burned to whorls.
Too tired to live, to die, to anything
kilned in skin.

Syzygy

A whirlwind in a Thrift Store assembles nothing
although it suggests a shape. A bowtie,
swung on air, flutters without function
because no neck is there.

There is no bleak coordinate
to rally the flags and flairs;
no hairy simpleness untwisted
when bras and socks litter ascending stairs.

Eyeglasses doubt their doing
(no matter how pinched and proud their glare)
when through their frames of hardened ether
can go no softened stare.

But a belch out of Brahma
that moves through our tube of voice
(no matter the nakedness of our stance)
can clear the spirit's molten soma
or club bright diligence to trance.

Red suspenders written by a finger
on some supple manikin we love
leaves a mental trace that lingers
far longer than any snapping does.

Yes, clothing is the vocab,
the richness of what's said,
the silken bounty of hot balloons,
the droll draperies on the bed.

But it is the Alpha and Omega
of eye and heart and ear
that fill out their airy outline
with the grammar of a dare.

Down to Earth

We've landed at the restaurant. Imagine that!
Plastic seats and an oiled eggplant head
Eating itself with a painted fork, with kerchief tucked in.

A feast! A feast of cow-skulls,
Staring and hard, a mad Egyptian emblem of "brief life."
Oh, I'd as leif

Noose my neck
On your oniony tongue and grief
As eat the bitter sprigs laid on my plaid plate.

The yogurty folds of melted milk-slugs
Slopped to a standstill, a yellow hill,
The maggoty disaster of a vegan salad!

Yet here we sit, the paralyzed pair,
Hump and stump,
Too drunkenly sober to ever get up.

Who but us has smashed our lives to pieces?
One piece, two pieces....
Oh, too many pieces to count or fix!

That one looks like post-war France, Maryland that;
All of our magic plans have gone
Back into the magician's black hat.

Timid rabbit, silent as me,
Already minced and brewed in the mulberry stew
You vomited in the bathroom—

Half an hour, and almost didn't come back.
Tell me, tell me,
One finger, or two?

How many hooks or claws does it take
To snake your guts into the toilet
And water your eyes awake?

Kimono Blow

Stirred eyes, lambent hands
Grope, stroke and lock
On the God-prod, the poker-pole, while red stone robes,
Judicial and exact, flow slow blood floods
From neck to heart to cock.

Your mouth moued to an exquisite squid
Flicks, sips and whips
The nodding blood-knot. Purple, imperial
Whirl unwrung above stung-hung nuts,
The daisy-anus, the lumped legs.

How like a heart it hurts,
Circular spurt and jerk
Into an emptiness of spit the size of a head,
Glow-globe toned with bruised velvets
And hot as a hiss or a piss.

This is the her that turned me twenty.
This is the act that soured all honey.
This is the night that cut away the day.
This is the feel that cancelled the real.
This is the time that mimed eternity.

Alive and dead on the slab again,
Burned, turned and horned
I made your waded pleasure feather wetness;
A fortune of fine-knit phillips ticked
Your broody veins insane on the scripted sheets.

Rumplestilskin

This hiss, this effortful fumbling at the spinning wheel,
A whirl of confused gold and one fine thread
Pure and tense as silence

Flies from the gnome's knobbed fingers that pull at the
    flow
Thin as a hummingbird's urine;
Masses of fineness

Gather at his neglected boots, clouds of extravagance
Churned from dirty straw.
And now

A maiden's motions move through the loops; pinching,
    stitching,
She weaves a molten cloak for His Majesty's child,
The sun king.

She uses every trick in the book to perfect it: her smile,
Her looks, her intricate skills, her willfullness
Honed on a husband of rock.

She shakes out the cloak. Millioned glimmers
Shiver down its breaking back. She's proud.
The gnome's eyes shine black.

"Magnifique! Too bad *your* son shall never have it."
Her face falls to scars, irritations.
Her eyes cross.

"Oh...oh...*Rumplestilskin!*" she cries
Into the surprised sound of silence.

Cannibal

Casual, usual
A face floats on its wavering stalk;
Look at it talk, talk, talk.

Watch it shimmer in the mirror
And dissolve, a tactless absence, a sore,
Hole for soul,

A nothing that wounds and wounds
With its teeth, its tongue, gassy solvents
That pick and ply til all's undone.

Look at it—loaded and goading,
A sucking contusion, wary and scarlet
Winking open only to eat

And eat and eat.
Watch how it swallows, grinding its stone molars
On a glass eye, a wooden heel,

Whatever the survivor had found
To replace itself with—a quick fix,
A snatch of branches, sticky love,

Any useable glue;
Anything at hand, at heart, anything
That would *do*.

The flaccid face bloats on its spoils.
Bigger than mirrors, it floats its way out.
Grandly, hatefully,

Empty of everything but plunder and hunger.

Narcotic Nirvana

A bhudda-man emerged in my dreams.
Orange sherbet draped his limbs,
His head a mahogany dollop.

His fist contained a shard, a glimmer,
Simple and sharp as his easy smile
That outshone his indigo eyes.

I held my palm up, outward, warding
Nothing, welcoming nothing,
A new-painted moon-palm with five drippy runs.

The knife
Entered me simply and neatly,
Dividing my five into a three and a two.

Sudden blood, hot and narcotic,
Glistened the fingered rifts of identity—and I, I
Bowed to thank him, kiss his head

The solemn mahogany
Made of my desire for death.

Cardiology

You hand me a cup, bland porcelain
Brimming with little liquids, little swirls
That mix without melding.

Edges meet my lips.
"Swallow."
A helpful hand wipes the excess with a damp cloth.

This medicine is steeped in piss-poison!
Injectable lies
That slide beneath the skin, scatter and assume

The airy shape of my veins,
My life-lines, and then coalesce in a tangle,
Intrude and lump in my heart, silk knot, waxy casket

That breaks in the calcified air
Displaying a dead baby,
A red statuette

Drowned by lies and poison, swimming in it!
O what shall it do, what shall it do
That once was innocent blue,

Clean and pure and crimeless as *you?*
Shall it lie in state, attended and indifferent,
Surrounded by suits and long faces,

The lamentable murmuring of men, the shriek
Of a mistress tearing her hair?
Or shall it rise, rouge moon, rise

Blind and on fire, and show us the night?
Show hidden things: faces twisted as paper,
Abominations, truces with witches,

Suburban ploys and plots, the adorable whores
Who live on the block?
If we look at it burning, the heart on fire

Will it show us just what we desire?
Will it show me? Will it show you?
Will it?
Will it?
Will it?

"One mated and angelic eve"

One mated and angelic eve
With the book flared across your knees,
Eyes guided eyes and elbows posed
For four brown nipples to squeak and see.

I knew the bell's praise from your lifted lips
Would sound my soul awake;
I knew each bit of bitch with a searing nail
Would seal my damaged fate.

Stiff ministers of a cultish creed
We repeated the stolen words,
Puked up tongue and black and naked need
Until our needing heard.

Together with stars and eyes half-open
We scratched the wrinkled skull's emporium
And traded hands and nimbly led
Each other back to bed.

"The voice that puts my world to worse"

The voice that puts my world to worse
Sits alien in the ear.
The juggling hand that hoists my heart
I exile to a hammered bier.

The eye that sees my face as sodden
I pluck and damn its tears.
The ear that hears my each word a curse
Whispers its own fear.

When that eye, that hand, that crooked ear
Misperceive my frame,
I crack each red rib and fish within
To kiss her soul again.

The Timid Leaper

"Sewn together in a pouch of purrs"

Sewn together in a pouch of purrs
Hand on breast and mouth on thigh
We cannot make our moaning words
Or hiss a thesaurus into our kisses' sighs.

Each sight of sex that turns us double
Or kinks or Xed zones to a core
Of double yolks where trapped tongues bubble
About the regions our mouths rub sore,

Undoes our encyclopedias of saying,
Erases summations to addition's first tick
And cancels accounts we could be laying
In the hollow of a kiss' lick.

~ 208 ~

Lyonesse by the Sea

O I have been to Lyonnesse
One hundred miles away;
I have been gone to Lyonesse
For many and many a day.

When I returned from Lyonnesse
Upon a rainy day,
I found my town and found my home
Had changed while I was away.

In what way all things had changed
I'd be hard-pressed to say,
But things that were things
    were no longer things
Since I had been away.

My regret is long
Where I once belonged
And hardly can I see
When the hours gong

What is left of what I've left
In Lyonnesse by the Sea
And what at home from where I'd gone
Is left of what has been.

Answering Machine Messages:

1]
Robbed of sleep I can only feel
The iron bed of your steel will
And sleepless lie upon my cot
Meditating over what I have not

2]
Although we don't know Reality's basis
Time is not a stasis
For (God knows) in Life's whirlpool
Each one goes from sage to fool

3]
"Thank you for breaking my heart, you sonofabitch"
You're Welcome, then
Is where we must begin
For the breaking of the heart
Is the very worst part

4]
her eyes a monster's beauty
her laugh contagious fire
her heart too finely lonely
her breath a wilderness of desire

During and After

The Yoni in her rictus sucks
Lingam with her million licks;
Like and unlike they dance and drain
The sense of sophistry and the heart of pain.

Glad carousels lunge where sex has lingered,
Whirling in memory what had been fingered;
The touch of Life that touches us
Commends us crawl above the dust.

Mandala Squalor

Put mandolins where monkeys are
To screech their souls up to a star

Bananas and citrons in a deep dish
Chocolate shadows and the sunlight's kiss

The revolved aroma of a hole
Charms the sense that would scold

Morning Moment

good morning
dear blossom,
the dawning's
white bosom

is clearing a place
for your health
for your face
whose smile is wealth

Naked Eloquence

Shards of naked eloquence,
permanent acquaintance in a glance,
an isosceles triangle constructed by chance
as when the world falls together
            on the disheveled bed.

Shapes of light and greatness
confound the eye to quietness
and all the rest as well, unless,
confessing naked eloquence
and stretched to a howl

I stand with my back
to the midnight clocks
and drop my cock
            to the caustic waters,
my soul to spawn.

Hollywoody

I stare at my figure
too dull to doll
it up with knots, wry ribbons
that stitch the wild hair into a tail.

The hips flare out
from the belly sack, a hairy flood
of becomings, selves
I may invite back for a drink…

Incipient breasts
flow molded from mounded shoulders,
nipples stiff to be bitten.

It's womanish,
except for the blowfish.

Figgy balls
complacent as labia, shed placenta
from some god-afterbirth.

The dill a willie
soft as a loaf or foggy forethought,
clitoral when licked

by a mind or a lip
anything that drugs the blood
into the long cave,

the manger
hung with drums, a terrified beating
that surges and squeezes.

A swallowed heart
would be less insistent, more nutritive,
provide a maturer moaning

than this hollow stick
with its found sounding, a seashell
dragging its echo.

Hot, prophetic
folds saunter simmer-shimmeringly,
lacteal, erect.

The wet coast
solders its salts against the groin,
sand and fire and thighs.

A night, a womb
floats her sewn awning over us,
a marmalade

softness constricted to eloquence.
Stars hung out to dry,
zen observers,

mark our dartings
like twins in the linen.
Love, love

swells and sweats
between us, cloisonné oysters
stripped

from their bone shells,
the shellac of evolution
returned to nudity.

Somewhere, hidden
below the neckline of waters
that define us,

my semen rot
and wait, rot and wait,
acid prisoners

pale to escape.

Scold

The face is porcelain, sourceless
perfection

towed from the cemetery
whites of the sea

and spit upon by lime,
cremated to this coldness, this clarity.

Blank statuette,
unriven by sweetness or sorrow,

smooth as a blind moon
or dew on a cactus!

Follicleless, is this
the end of wrath and worry?

Does a wild rabbit shred cries
below your shine?

Anatomy entrapped by a sheen,
mechanism steeled to a polish,

there are such depths in your surfaces!
A star could not finish it.

No sun
can blanche you beyond what you are.

Limitless
glares anger at you larynx

that never once hurt open for air.
How does it feel to be in there

seamless and beaming? Tell me, tell me!
Open your mouth and bleed

a God-spout,
a riot.

Mister S

The scenery of the ribs is a stage-set:
medieval coils of veins,

cracked flames
and the abysmal bellows,

the gold heart going like a pocket-watch,
muffling a photoed face in its hands.

Heart! O Heart!
Look at the ruins you have maneuvered!

the hothouse monster who smashes the panes
and leaves the scene in spasms.

Mysteries
stiffen the pinions

of God's black bat,
dark Lucifer, soiling the filigree paneling

as he loiters, fingering a silk cigarette.
He's plausible,

a skirmish of smokes and dishwater, lonely
for a light or a toke....

A molten, mirrory backdrop
floats his eyes through the chest like train-lights;

A few, stray, unused thoughts
flashing and dangling

assemble the scarecrow
who puts goodness to flight.

Hole for Soul

I keep falling into holes
and trying to stay there.—*Theognis*

Holes split open like smiles,
wet and black as a line of paint,
full of spectacular textures, like current berries
that cling to my fingers, to my
hounding mouths, to my wicked dick.

My pubes are adorned with the hard small seeds,
spit out and germed with turmeric jelly.
The hairs stand forth bright as a bearing holly bush,
gemmed like a juniper with seeds and needs.
And there, nearby,
like the sand at the end of the slide,
hunkers the hole, the sop, the punch-out,
bitch ditch and oblivion
as final as an out-push of breath.

I have fallen a thousand thousand times
tripped by a mirrory eye, a laugh,
the sudsy tug of an insult,
a breath as coal and nitrous as a cigarette,
smokes that exit a sigh as silk exits a spider's belly.
I have heard and I have fallen.
I have seen and I have slipped.
Again and again, in and in,

Down and down I go, shucking my parachute
into crowded clouds, removing my wiry limbs

to increase my speed
into the fishy abyss, the feathery cleft
that opens like the vowels of a moan
in the middle of a woman.

There's an arm, a foot, a useless
knee as backwards as a bird's,
an ass as smooth as a cameo
unrolling and unreeling.
Clothes shudder off like smoke.
I am leaving it all behind
like a will or a fire sale,
getting rid, getting rid,
to fit into this hole that opens below,
black and silk
as a magician's hankie.

Faster and faster I fall
my hat pulled off in a flap and flutter,
my head yanked back like a yo-yo.
Springy fingers twine my greasy curls.
The angels go on about light and space and eternity
like a clean room that never dirties,
linen and palm trees and Ikea settings that never end
fresh as dry cleaning,
airy and forever and empty.

But I want the hole.
I want that plummet of gums,
the chummy manure of descent,
that spasming black, that tongue of hunger,
the window in my stomach screaming wide,
the tears, the million million tears
like bent nails, bent and abandoned

from nailing the window open, again and again
to feel the black rising though you
as you fall.

Surgery

What are we made of who made ourselves?
Our hands pull at the stitches like petals
"love me, love me not"
until our lovable monster lies
undone and red and ruined
as a pile of raw scarves.

Quick, quick, take these flicked cracks,
the ones under the brows and by the eyes,
or the one jaggedy one as long as a sigh
long and nipple-purple by the targeted heart
and pinch it and knit it and tie a tight knot,
knowing that the guts have already gone out of it,
the heaving mongrel mess
the contusions and bruises
and god knows what
that make us human and helpless and work.

Where our kisses have stung
a rosary of burns remains;
What had happened back when the lightning struck
and love arose? What surged and gurgled
on the steel table? What awoke with a shock to see
the operating room's sugary whites,
the corners as sharp as a smirk?

What shuddered and blinked
at the rubber and tubular helper hands
so anxious to gag it and glue it,
to take it to us and keep us together

like a heap of busted toys in a box?
The surgical light as intense as a sty
blinked on above us like a faulty halo.

Notice the choosing of the bones,
the supple back, the wavery feet,
the bland big bone of the face, blank as a lollipop.
Notice the choosing of the bones,
very important and very proper,
stark popsickle sticks stuck in two frozen lives,
rounds and mounds to hang ourselves on,
display our guts like sausages
and our smiles like carved lard.

Bellwether

This is the husband, a stone Ramses head
indifferent and flecked with flies, with lies, austere as the
    sunset
that gilds his despair.

He's different, this husband, he's changing
songless and bald, moulting his plumage
undoing his hues.

Long ago he finished with sending me poems,
his pen as dry and stark as a husk.
Done are the days of ripping the earth

to snare me a fist of flared flowers
that peeped, in our noontime,
so "naive et charmant" from my ratsnest of hair.

Eons back he shut himself off like a faucet
from my teasing yeast,
my rise as regular as the calendar.

He no longer cries in straight silver lines,
stopped are the drops once poignant as blood.
His tongue is no longer a spongeable pumice

to leaven or sharpen my sex upon.
Turned off are the nights of spasms and gladness,
torn away like kites by unbearable thunder.

The Timid Leaper

Stoked stiff in his study with his load of self-pity
he chugs through his Churchill in his stagnant recliner,
a thrumb drubbed on Nietzche, and a pinky in Zeno,

dividing and slicing our lives into zeroes.

Shine

This is the scrape and scar of disarming sin,
The God scrub.—
Filtered pallors hurricane the holy void

Empty and innocent
And quite as frank as an open mirror or storm-eye.
Oz-God with his cattle prod

And tanned hands replete with treats
Tells us in Schonenberg tones
We must wash or wear out.

Old hopes, old hands, old wings
Weaken and retard my rinsing and rising;
What held me up now halts me.

My father's feathers that lightened my marrow
Now endow my face with suffocation
As thick as Icarus' kisses.

All these withered glimmers and subtle shines
Impinge and peel off in the mud;
All Earth is crowded with 'down.'

And I, I rise in rain
My high lungs two cauldrons of flammible gold,
My hope as strong as a bird's hollow bones.

The Soft Assault

A scream arrives
as eloquent as a silent film,
Chaplin eating his shoe from hunger,
us eating our screams from love.

Has it been so long since
our mouths had found the strength
to swim at each other like fish and kiss?
Water whooses from our guts into water,
urine and fishshit deflating from us,
the sound a no-sound of silence.

So long and so hungrily we moved toward each other,
paired plants heliotroped on our sunny dope
and ache for greatness, a spine of thorns
elevating the ticklish emptiness of a rose.
I cared for no God taller than your caress,
your hot neck caught on my calluses.

The crevices where we creased together
like folded skin melted in a blue matchstick
are full of crossed eyes and crossed hairs,
backwards assassins
that cannot see what they are killing
but fumble for the tricky trigger by habit
blindly as worms.

Together we mouth the sound of "Pow"
like children
pulling their fingers on air.

Reincarnate Incarnate

I have come and gone many times
And turned my soul upon a rhyme
As if the finest joke on earth's
To be always beginning where I was.

Troubled troubadour and truculent whore,
Soldier, sailor and tailor and more;
Each rotating mood or face
Another fated deck shot by an ace.

The several major arcana and their signs
Cast their shadows on my soul;
Sour and sweet they they cross and meet
And their friction boils my bones.

Bird or man or querlous bee,
Or gladdened tangle of these three I am stuck on
Winter's blankest branch
Or come to Summer's triumphant tree:

Hung, flung, or even undone
Our lives' alliance shifts upon a breeze
Straying or staying like some mourner's melody
Upon the upright mystery.

With ignorance and assurance I strut;
With innocence and wickedness I walk;
With whatever measure I may I go;
Indisputable and bouyant I stalk.

Mother shadow and darkest seed
Direct from the nothing above
And sink to the nothing below
All the lightness that I may need.

Cajoling aueroles of flowers
From these honey-bloods I bleed
Dripped to ground beyond my powers
Until light and time a resurrection freed.

Calliopes' sighs and a lover's tropes
Rope my myriad thoughts to things;
Tied together what need I fear
Save a lesser tension in the strings?

I have come and gone many times
And turned my soul upon a rhyme
As if the finest joke on earth's
To be always beginning where I was.

Oblivion Vignette

So circular evening arrives again
Sending down her silver lies at midnight
Into the sleeping mind of woman,—
A goddess knotted on her own fecundity,
A fullness and dirtiness in which all fantasies root.
My blunt foot has numbed in its soleless boot.

And yet, there is no anchor for us in this evening,
No hold, no place to contain us,
To comfort us; no chink in which we may
Fail and be forgotten. No hole for our seeding.
We are here in the evening alone together,
Here in the bleak nothing that opens us.

I look up, up, to where the black stops.
The stars are wise of their taut untruths
And wink when we do stare at them,
Staring like a mother at her liar child
Who winks and grimaces and starts away
To play and pleasure in the darkest wood.

Dissembling Earths:
Addenda And A Conclusion

Praying Out Loud to the Earth

Vouchsafe my voice may its voyage make
beyond closed body, its closets and its coughs;
and may my uncertain meaning sweeten,
and my white intention leaven
whatever hoarfrost horror might roughen
or conspire with sliding Time to take.

When your look alights, so soulfully open,
my syllables Philippic to protest,
each cabinet burst, their vacant emptiness.
So hollowly they go your full gaze along,
a skinny whistling wind round gravid earth,
I moan with thinness where you stand strong,

a willess whisper strained across a mountain's growth.
So you uphold me wherever I go
—an errant profligate invisible above
(whose forgotten as soon as sighed), and who blows
himself to nothing to herald aloud
how the green solid world unfurls below.

The Golden Ticket

Little mattered, and much pervaded
The antique living room too much sunlight had
    degraded;
A little heartache burned beneath his cassock,
And holy daybreak shattered at the blinds.

If Christ defied his fashions
And strode untemplated and rude,
If Hitler really killed them all
Then how dare I intrude?

My voice imparts and falls, toils and tolls,
Its happenstances and romances, its passions
Its trances of a certain evening in a certain loll
And on into dawn prepares some further wrong
Inconsequent, yet beckoning, a passionate
Lark backspread against dispassionate clouds.
(I have stood upon the Arctic zones and poles
Of certain yellow unlighted rooms.)
Among the wasted cigarettes and torn pornography
I have sifted and resisted so many
Facts and truths that harshly glare in so many
Wasted one-time afternoons.

Holding, holding
Our hands beneath the spider's pall were golden.

The hackneyed painter's ennui endures
Formulas of snow and absence, building sets;
Nailed in the aurora's tonic light, and stiff,
My red shoes stand steadied on a cliff.

(I sew my fingers backward that sew my shroud.)
And I have wandered lost and wondered found
And in a crossed broken shadow drowned;
(I have lived my life while floating upon the rood.)

Chastized eyes
Chastized eyes
Glare no more on inward wars
Accreted dusts that sharply crept
Down the pale defiles at midnight,
Or assembled dust tumbled from untouched dresser
    drawers
Spilling golden dirty light over all.
(I have seen them all, and touched them all
And thrown them all away already,
Golden crowns cascading to a wastebin.
I have touched the molten blots that blot within.
I have rearranged my clothes upon a hook.)
Here's some argument's half-misapprehension,
There, the moronic posture of a gesture
Gilding the broken indices of fate.
A look, a moment's condescension
Gazes back from above a moth-eaten bureau
To fall upon the blankness of a wall.

And I have longed and I have lounged,
Taking nights apart to tack the day together,
And still the terrorist dawn arrives, inflicts
Green and golden, and obliterates my weathers.

O fol de rol de rolly o
My bloodless feet are skirled in skeins of snow

Daybreak snaps the blinds. Bored, it leaves
Out through exhausted windows where I have thrown

How many tired glances into airs unknown?
And they are tired, emptied by seeing,
Glancing netherwhere, seeing, recoiling,
Seeing the thousand toiling hours of neglect
The glazed eyes of weary aspect,
Hollow yet disdainful, and rolled upon a bulb
Or blindly churched in the long, squared
Eternity of a ratty book that blazes
Trashed Byzantiums in footnotes obscure;
Or restless finds itself still climbing
To some even more forgotten shelf
While a quaint, antiquarian transcendence
Cool and numb
Floods moldy light upon the moldy carpeting.

And still the snow inquires
And still the day expires
Answerless, if my foot shall daedalus the fresh.
(I have killed and I have died for less.)

—No, no I haven't been. Is it near here?
What's it like? Is it extraordinary?

       Oh, its full
Of quiet shades, thoughtful darknesses.

—My, there's no end to things in the heart.
Is there now? Now is there?

No, no truly;
There is never any end to things.

And the squeeze of nights, the evenings
Where so many eden days have sank entranced,
Collapsed so charmingly about an aborted heart

In so many unheated ochre rooms alone!
Oh I have seen and mourned the fabled light
Disastered in a rucksack crease of dirty pants.
And yet, how shall I begin, and how beget?
I have looked through ochre eyes and hollow rooms
Undeceived, and yet, and yet....

I am scarred and I am mastered in the garden,
Near the wisteria, iced by the moonlight's
Porcelain glances. How many years and days
Has it been, how many, since first, in moonlight,
We traded sudden glances?
Roses had maddened us, and we were glad.
Here, balancing the wisteria on a fingerend
Pointing past my agile nose to oblivion,
Cold leaves rustle in the ruined fountain;
Water's memory in the concrete bowl
Scratching over the water's ancient course.
A thousand points of light conflict
In a thousand parted dooryards;
Conflict, flicker, and then resolve
Focused into a single momentary glow.

(My eyes and I contain
A thousand portions of a thousand parted souls.)

O fol de rol de rolly o
My bloodless feet are skirled in skeins of snow

Summery Elegy

The crayon-crammed sun, dear,
Roaring and soundless, fountains
A crooked rivering stalk to the grave
For it is summer and never
Among the milkweed floods of grass
Will everyday angels flame again
Dawn wise and luminous as thread
Out of the martian mysterious dark,
—So tall was the flying sunshine
Spied in your crinkled eyes.

The milky sun hung up the sour day,
With daylong hands played the harp grasses
That plucked our praise-soaked ears
There on the floor of light
For it was summer and ever
Our milk-licked unmanageable bones
Pounded joy and adoring down
The auroraed roughs of our breaths
Till silk-dripping souls announced
Heaven commences at our fingertips.

Oh it was dawn and noon, and night
Dropped his forgotten trunk of darks
Among the staggered stars as I came,
The sun's brother, halogened as haloes
Shining my wary wishes in the air
For it was summer come and never
In the pearly rivers of the grass,
Will I silk my grabbing eyes again

On the welcome-at-once loving
Of your eiderdown sighing skin.

Now ambergris and matchless
The mirage-trod moon emerges like a tear
Over a mourning soul simple as sleep.
And because summer is overthrown
And night has leapt up like a cat
Under the harp-tongued tree of cells
My vegetable hand now grows
Mannerly and large to grief:
O Time has denied me nothing
Of his liquorice whips and nickels
Nor eboned one nightfall or fastness
Shut on your ghost-wasted alien eyes.

Pulled by the spoken tide of the clock
At midnight moonless rest I writhe
Resplendent in my bent vest of ribs
And hear both tomb and rumour tumbled dumb
By the mild handmaidens of your sighs
For it is summer gone and hollow
And sorrow's gone down with the moon
And though I tongue earth's dust floods
For all those romancing eyes gone under
Fate's timeline is still the grass on fire
Burning where the wood was wild.

And the crumpled sun, broken, bears
Funeral tears in the brain
That wombwise and graveward crawl
Down the fiery alcoholic face
For it was never summer or was it
Under my coal-thumbed universal eyes;

And only the bigsouled sourceless moon
Drowned and void in the jailhouse dark
Remains and grieves derailed sighs
Over night-locked trees tall as grasses.

Do not grieve, brave, with whys
Nor hemorrhage one ear with a sigh;
No heavenhelp salves such ashes.
O Let instead the dear uncandled dead
Cry mercy up to my eyes.

So I might suffer

So I might suffer without fail the vengeance of leaves
Crumbling, vein by vein, to the docks of autumn's
dust
And burn again in a rasping year
My fled blood
Both woke and broke
Flood and voice over the sea-turning town.
So that the wail of the crickets might knock and
enter
Each sad shadow passage of the pulse
I woke
Burning in the shining rivers that skip out of sight.

In the helping hurt of the one-armed weather
Flinging hailstones and adders
Down the ocean-thieving tunnel of the sky
Against this head
I swore all summer dumb
While the ministering crickets in the booming grass
Chanted phylums of my blood about to be said
And I stood in the summer's drum
Surrounded
By the roaring going of the year.

Ignorant of thistlery we walked in our mystery
Arm in arm like the burning boughs
Friends against death in the summer's long breath,
And like the sun we sauntered

Drunk and wandered
Through the closed book of the heart;
And I was sky and sunlight in the chapters of the
grass.
And understanding
I sang:
Oceans in acorns my strumming mermaids are.

Socketless and Sailor

Socketless and sailor
In the world's winded veins
Scented genesis and coffinsilk
I mock the soberest cockerel
Diving from the prism-spitting
Pinnacle of the world's mast
Uselessly singing
And rant like a wronged girl
All my sweetest notes
Over ignorant houses
Slumbered in death and morning light.

Out of the closeted shout this echo beats
Features of a sinning man on tin
More pressed to anguish in a dial's sigh
Than any victim of time heretically cried
Has been bludgeoned by suns
Or a pauper's bliss been
Crimped in a penny's fear
Or any tale of the world
Cauled in a scorpion's sting
Has twisted its smile on a man's side
Or any climbed tirade
Spoken in wishes
That nature's weary fabulist
Set down.

Graveturning in wishes
As a wish is a kiss
My manbones shriek

In blooded inks
Out of a rage welled and calmed
As any bird's ratcheted turn
Over the thumbing sea at dawn
Crawls at clouds
In inching desire as each wingbeat clips
Over measured cessations
Chewing ships and bones to flour.

Out of each brick
The cold dawn shakes
And each root tooth of daisies
Cragged in the fingering spring
Floods pulse and fever
To ramshackle gods agog
As saints in whispers
Each aghast their closed wings keep
Singing of statuary
And the boiling joy
Of the devil's boyish kiss.

So I this saintly mort cry down
And each nailed lip kiss
Quagmired in hatred
Tried and hung, on pentecostal cross and hatch
Birthing the blood plant
Insisting in stitches
For this world the word's wound.
So I, crumbling on windfall,
On sold bones and the tarot told
Watch hatred disaster, man and god fall,
And all loved things end.

Oh Let the Light Be Broken

Oh let the light be broken
That soaked and solemn
Out of the sun's mouth spoken
Climbed the virgin's hide
And the grave of her face.
Be buried in the stolen stone
Each word of sight
That from the tongue's priested
Memory is severed
Hunkered in the seed of the cold.
Oh let the light be broken
Over shackled genesis
Until the husks have spoken
Word and weed and sizzling stem
Out of the grave of her face
Alive again, and the once burning
Turn of the world
Stumbles back to ochre.
Let man and woman and infant dread
Out of harrowed heart
Lain long and solemn
Step from the narrow incision
Speaking in leap years
The carved distresses
Scourged in the drop of a tear's face
Hanging and grieving
After its home of fruit
Under bruited tree
Bruised and fishnet against the sky

The Timid Leaper

Solemnly detached as a leaf's face
Ghosted on stones
Waiting for the last hanged man
To dive alive at last.

The Silence

On undemanding ground
Shot through with hollow sounds
Bird or bullet make
Or some other keen cry, I take
This man for model, though in truth
A small man of the town; and although
His grandfather was a thief
And his father worse than that,
I respect his grief, for what else can I
That wander in the clay?

There was a man had died
Frozen to the mountainside
And, nothing in his climbing pack
And less upon his withered back,
He ascended the wintry peak
Sang a rich bar tune and died.
It was out of pride
The old man had died.
He gripped a flute, knew God's great lie,
And had a clarity in the eye.

And at the last, a damned wretched gaiety
Suffused his frame.
Mountain echo upon echo
Hollowed out his fame;
Dying, trying once again
To empty himself of troubles by the score—
"This joy of death
Stops the breath."

In the trees, excited laughter;
And after, the silence.

Dead

What has life's bitter disappointment brought
Laid in a narrow, breathless bed?
Shall we curse all our drunken, muddy lot
Lain with long bones of the dead?

At the end of a rifle or parting stream
Pursued by a pursuing dream
Man wakes up to find his enemies again,
The end of dreams, and all friends dead.

What stays hid in the marrow there,
Thrust deep underground?
Things purposed in the unpurposed air
Die when those men are dead.

Whether father or brother still pursue
Their work, or others' work, I do not know;
I read it on a narrow, upright stone
Cast by the long bones of the dead.

Fathers sacrifice long-loving sons
To a nameless, breathless bed;
Stand we under an island sun
Or lie with long bones of the dead?

Psalm 1

Oh, language, why have you left me
and tongue why have you forsaken me?
The waters of my mouth are as a rock.
My words are a fountain that no longer runs
the clouds of my eye are dry.
The fields of my being are burnt to stalks,
their verdure lies shocked and degraded.
I am shucked and hollow only now.
That which flowed through me is now fled.
Cisterns in my lungs deep with bowls of meaning
lie emptied and shattered; they are dead.
My soul has walked under the eves of despair
and stepped into a shadowy place.
The shapes that beheld my hands
now are fled as in a broken dream;
chance sentences and meaningless accents
appall the day worse than the most wretched silence.
The new time of the morning no longer glorifies me,
afternoons are hot, confused with musings;
I am no more a thing to myself without you, o song!
a dead man wrapped in today's living,
a whisper that cannot hear itself.
Time indulges the spectacle, space adheres;
temptation that once so strongly bade me onward
like new dress laid out before me
folds soiled and dusty before my sense.
Chance and disaster, my twins,
bring nothing, are bright in nothing, come to nothing;
they are sold and dead, unmournable whores.

The mountain from which I saw myself, and perceived
    love,
as doves perceive it in the tilled field,
the open homes quaint with chimney smoke,
is flattened and ashes now. I am nothing and nowhere
a traveler with no goal for his feet,
a melody without purpose, hissed to a screech,
an arrow without target or trueline—
misery without meaning, despite double sadness,
a low moment stubbornly remembered,
without reason, without fixtures, like an old scald.

Psalm 2

Sweet willing water of my mother's body
why have you left me here?
My heart once so vivid and precious within me,
is now incased in sand. The thoughts of my father
are as strangers to me, unbidden and unwelcome;
we never traveled very far together.
Sleepless sour frowns on my muse's face
create ignorant clouds inside me.
Streams rush by battling, happy and buoyant,
while I stand aside. Leaves crack into fruit,
my blossoms have never hardened or matured,
they orbit ignorance and ecstasy irrelevantly.
Maddening ruts follow their own roads nowhere.
The seasons cringe into change. I, larval,
wallow in wasteful wonder bewilderingly;
my body is the scrapped habitat of apes,
the single plume of a doomed bird: an ostrich, an eagle.
the razors of my eyes have told to dullness,
and are bloodied and blunted,
numb with too many things. The water
is at my feet; my feet are cool
in the growing roll of water, laughed at
and comforted are the ankles. The walk is easy;
the knees are held lightly, shining-weighing.
And now my lungs are stamped with the new motion.
A heavy mercury, bright and without mercy,
holds the muses' potent time, a cadence
against teeth, increasing in loveliness,

and sufferers into the appellate gullet
like a cold breath, an endless spurring.

Psalm 3

Cool is the gravestone laid by for thee,
Soft is the expected Ariel that confounds thee
whose wings awakening with the light
are a memory, a daydream without curse
fragrantly remembered, new moan hay in the nostrils.
Night with its many clouds has come,
day still waits to arrive;
thinking of nothing I have crept into a collar,
diamond-deeded and deified…these thoughts
counsel closely as fast friends,
I am cinched in.
When the angel of longing tramples desire,
when dust is with us and green grass is not,
when fear is with us and assurance is lost,
how may we recover forever?
Day comes with its ray's visit and raillery,
long walks in your yard empty of thought.
These ears have continued hearing
long rivers of unpolluted wine.
These eyes are victims saying all.
Howl! How may I be made fit for life
who is so misshapen? whose mirror is a question-mark?
I feel the wing of Ariel and have touched the hot hoof!
[How long and literal are your ages, Desire!]

My skin slits from its default.

Each sense sits configured for glory, again,
each moment made a mandible to apprehend,
each cherry converted to a church to enter.

With sapience and with praise I enter,
with blood on my righthand,
with heaven on my shoulder,
with bones in my sorrow,
with wind as my base and wickedness my tower,
the smile of dust and with a brow of Love,
I enter this somersault I have been dealt.

Psalm 4

All these years walking and where have I got to?
Looking before me I see advancing troubles,
looking behind me I see the nothing dust,
feel the cold pouring down my neck....
to the left a man looking down and still walking:
icy regret and old habitations.
To the right, that which I desired and have forgotten.
Looking down, I see my feet and what they might have
    been;
looking up, I see the judgment not withheld....
Glancing back within myself
will some strange being not return my stare?
Inside—inside I sense the blessings and the bliss,
some silver shadow of my desiring unsullied.
Steeped with ferocious being burns my happy littleness;
within is the crown unconquered!
What a man desires of the while, who will gainsay?
What voice will arise in the world's opinion
and with that opinion whip him?
My foot has gone upon a triple tread:
looking backwards and forwards and inwards,
each pace has placed me three places at once.
Tears, and salt of pain, anxiety and trepidation,
pave the mortal manner of my advancement.
What will slow my going or disable my loitering?
What will my speed achieve?
When the mountains rear tomblike with their snow
how will the saying sky stay silent then?
When the eyes look lions but no heart slays

and the bones of fire and age are upon us,
who will court his recollection to remember
what miracles we had put into our years?
When action and touch and art are temptation no longer
will cold and cold attract us
among the millions of moments and maybes?
Who will achieve even unto the limit of a single breath?

Coda
When the oracle discourses with the dunce
there can be no God.
When a brave man is framed by his fears
or the coward surveys in hope the majesty of his grave,
there can be no God.
When a priest is used to plea with the blast
there can be no God.
When the populace is swooning for holy approbation
there is no God.

Outing

No Transcendental Impulse but then
Invaded, sense by sense, and sense by sense again!

Confused, harassed, stammering, half-mad,
I arrived at a mountain stream's small source alone
Whose each more moment of dropping flowing
By dropping more intensely flows. Heart's-blood
Stuttered along the tongue of solvent air
Following out the stream's wanderings apace
As if my liquid's hush through every cataract
And canyon-enhancing rivulet did move;
What weariness then penetrated every limb
Which had flung itself the whole blue morning through
Like a ceaseless wheel! I lay a lonesome hour
Upon a tabs of stone spined just so long
As myself from dead heel to skull-top
Imagining its travel! By my veins
The moss-indentured rook with iron force
Is cracked, a hammering flow enveloping the mass
With pale empurplings and smooth-prompting bulbs of
    glass
That maturer nature had given a more rugged touch.

So I lay sun-warmed upon that human stone,
Neither foot nor head beyond its grating cradle,
Until all that made me I un-made
Then wove again together in eye and ear;
As if sunlight spoke and sound gave voice in light
All these before me in hazeless dazzle floated free
And I consigned them to their Liberty!

My rushing emerging blood swept past
Cochlea and ear-drum in bird-like thrum:
Stream on stream ascended purer air in song
Til all was bathed by part, the unaccustomed whole
Of oceans leaping from my spring! each martlet that sang
Told some note of me; myself had stained
Sky's unstarred majesty with pinks, and in a wink
Sent each sense sharpened as ft spread
From azure zones of whispered fire
To the old pond's own cool shadow of repose
Til every busy sound was somewhat tinged with red
And every shifting leaf, dew-shadowed as they were,
Burned outlined by that bright delight
Their own laughing motion shucked from them in
      sound.

Then a purple rain, it seemed, descended
In answering haloes shaken from the sun
And broke in its descent to mist hallowing all.
No part of the under-sky receded
From that pursuant touch,—but rather
Rose to its own undoing in erotic rapture
As drones to their honey-loving maiden-queen
Lift translucent wings in flight;
Leaf and leaf in murmuring applause
Stretched on each twig-end toward that sky!
The stone that held my casing seemed more up-raised
And the low appearance of the swimming sun
Took on a duskier and a closer tone
As if it wished to immerse itself again!
Strange mist was everywhere, endowing each
Glowing glen that lay as little as a lens.
Strange mist had wrapped the very bowsprit of the rock!
My own skin was mist-engrafted!

Within, my own departing heart,—
So whirled with-in and-out with the luminous,—
—As pulsant globe and center now resolved.

And on this thought my mind no longer moved,
By spells of rapt intransigence inly held,
Til all that had its faultless action once impelled
Conjoined to conjure pause; sweet was the wind
That kissed my aching lungs with such sweet breathe
All piny, with some sunny hawthorn scenting mixed,
—Even still that air is fresh within me,
Even still do I desire the clearness I had then!—
For one hour's welter of such unwon wealth!—
For then I had found out—in clearness still
Do I see it!—motive of moon and sun and sincerer stars,
Our perpetual guest, the unsullied source of glory
That limned my out-flowing veins in rivers'light!
Out, out of the very center where my spirit slept
Flood called out to flood and flood responded
Out-pouring Life! there, there are the harmonies!
There the endless systems counted back to One!
There the measureless Space contented
To a water-drop! There echoings on echoings
By their velvet source are hushed!
Anguish and insistence vanquished by a touch!
Nightmares and chimeras chastized by a love
The soul's own shaping power makes animate!

The Bookshelf:
BLAST PRESS Offerings

http://www.corporategreed.com/gregglory
  gregglory@aol.com

All Titles only $2.50 each (includes postage). A bill will be sent along with your poesy book. Read and enjoy—with confidence!
Some Other Titles in the BLAST PRESS Catalogue are:

THE POET'S ONLY VISION

IT'S THE SEX PISTOLS

YOUTH YOUTH YOUTH

CONTEMPORARIES

ULTRA

TORTURED SPLENDOURS OF THE DREAM

THE BOOK OF E

DIVINE REVOLT

ADORING THORNS

SEVEN HEAVENS

THE ROSE LASSO

XXX SONNETS

THE CABANA AT THE EQUATOR

THE DOLLAR GOD

PROMETHEUS BOUND

LOUIS B. LIPCHINTZ ABANDONS SHIP

DR. KILMER'S OCEAN-WEED HEART REMEDY

A CREDENT REGALE

AUTOBIOGRAPHIES; ESSAYS AND INTRODUCTIONS

AUTOBIOGRAPHIES; DEUS ABSCONDIS

THE DEATH OF SATAN

EVERLASTING ARCHANGELS

ANTIGONE; SOPHOKLES RESSURECTED

CONSTELLATIONS IN DECEMBER

BURNING BYZANTIUM

ASCENT

RED BANK

REFUTING HUME

All Titles only $2.50 each (includes postage). A bill will be sent along with your poesy book. Read and enjoy—with confidence!

FROM: THE POET'S ONLY VOICE AND VISION:

Rimbaud wanted LIBERTY in salvation. But one is only saved by surrendering this illusory freedom.—Henry Miller. How much wrongness can ONE inanity comprehend? Miller's definition of liberty is skewed, and maybe Rimbaud's agreed with Miller's (making him skewed too—but I don't think so).

To want LIBERTY in salvation is entirely correct. But what one wants, of course, is meaningful liberty. And what gives this liberty meaning for us is for that individual liberty to have an immense impact on our neighbour, for it to manifest in the free and true hearts of others who, free themselves, may register such liberties freely.

Miller pretends that Rimbaud only wants the liberty to ACT as he wished, sans context, with or without contact with the rest of the human race.

FROM: IT'S THE SEX PISTOLS!!!

Prologue

[To be spoken by Lester Bangs, Richard Hell, or Griel Marcus.]
We gather here some summers past his death;
The air near us bears its sweet fragrance yet
As in the dim past it was accustomed
To have borne. We come to document a trial
Of youth, and speed, and the chase of fire
That edges young veins anxious yet to burst
The bare confinement of the body.
Ambitions churned in mills of desperate hope,
And clear vision upreared from smoky tenements
Crouch within our subject's city-bounds as well.
Everything not incidental
To a prince's birth in loathed ashes
Shall be told in what we are about to speak:
Mire costuming here a spirit as rare
As any that went naked in greater ages
Whose philosophers, incidents, and strange tales
Whisper still in books passed down to us.
He was one—I cannot speak it—but let
Him show; he was one to tumble Jove

Or put into the gestures of his peers
Antics to mimic truth out of hiding
And mock empty vaunt with its own faces.
He was as Michaelangelo's god of boys, set down
In despite of time, vaunting, vague,
A fishing rod as able in his white fist
As any furling sling to draw tyrants down.
Now I before your gentle selves appear
And ask you reconstruct from rended memory
This man, whose trim vitality works wonders
In us yet; who, as though king among those ghosts
We are yet to join, he captains our resolve
And sails us, briefly parted, to those parts
And kingdoms of ourselves we quail to glance at.
Let one summer stand for millions,
And let a universe of lives be exampled by
One life, one death. It is fair enough.
Let not identity struggle besmirched in the mass
Or roil in the crowding roll of oceans
Of limbs—so like a war is any hived
Metropolis. Instead let concentration fall
From our high heaven of observation
Into the single life and particular fate
Of our chosen hero. Let him be unveiled:
[Spotlight comes up on Sid, biting a hangnail.]
You see he fits the mold, but not how well;
That is the office of our tale to unfold
—And, if you will but tailor your wide
Imaginations to our narrow telling,
Refining in mind what our rush of detail
Must leave gross, and fitting yourselves
Into the garment of our object here
As if the skin of the protagonist
Himself, flushing round what was left in need
By the author's drying pen, we shall succeed.
Let us, and him, find what name will fit him best:

Paul: Sid!

FROM: YOUTH YOUTH YOUTH (A collection of Early Verse)

Sequence

1. Somnambulance
The mourning does are lying in leaves
For summer bleats and funeral ash.
Somewhere shipwrights are planning for ghosts.

2. Aftereffects of Silence
Singing, I thought there was a second
Voice behind me.
Only one dove was bowing.

FROM: CONTEMPORARIES

Saddam Huissain

"The petty strut of a peacock without a tail,
or old men salaaming for drachma in the city's dust,
so much scratching and disturbance of dust…
so much strafing and raping of the holy villages….
Here, year adds on to year, the camel chews as slow.
Lifted from the dung fire by a ladder of assassinations,
I climbed to kindle the deserted palace steps, and turned
my unerring hand to the populace, coaxing to vex
my nomad volk towards foam. Oily dollars,
skin thin, flutter as bats to the waste horizon
returning at motor dawn in the hunched shapes of tanks;
sea-anxious to return to the yaw and abyss of the sea,
Kuwait halts our monumental, crawling foot
and whines for a beach-badge from their simmered
verge of sand.
I pet a captive's infant before the camera, swill
the thick wine of Peace Through Annexation and stoop

in my ill-fitting soldier's fatigues to plead or command:
Surrender to God, whose white hand works through my hand."

FROM: ULTRA

ULTRA'S FIRST STATEMENT TO THE AUDIENCE:

I stand naked in front of you.
I can't lie to you for one second.
This is my story you will see.
I see it as one of redemption, Justice.
But how you will see it,
my thousand eyes transfixing this darkness,
I do not know, and I cannot say.
I only know that you have entered it, my story.
You will feel it in my blood as I feel it.
I do not accept that any distance can exist between us.
Not any distance in space.
Not any distance in culture.
Not any distance in time.
Not any distance in language.
Not in blood. Not in hope.
You are me, in this.
Who you will be afterward even you do not know.
I stand naked in front of you.
I can't lie to you for one second.
Oh, my thousand eyes,
my thousand eyes....

FROM: TORTURED SPLENDOURS OF THE DREAM

Hia! his tittering heart jumps to trumpets,
sighs to the bright sea-chanteys of rude, red men
that round the singing table and splitting boards
circle the singing sailors as they sing.
So finger down the Dorian lyre

from its dusty peg, and if
remotest Pisa can fling up
remembrance fit to each miracle, welcome
each one with presto phrases of your acutest twang.
And if that fine arabian, Pherenikos,
clips along Alpheos' magic stream, racing
unspurred inches of his dainty auburn flank
to vault the cantered body of his Lord
deep into the grip of winning,
resign then the wandering passions of your mind
to the emblazoned graces of his sparking hooves.

FROM: THE BOOK OF E

EVERYONE knows how absurd the project of philosophy is. But, having once acknowledged this generous absurdity, this insistent complexity of facts and life's sinuous situations, let us proceed nevertheless to open our mind's eye to the good doctor's medicinal drops. After the initial blunt distortions and pain of the sun, often so intense as to necessitate the donning of a cheap green filter for the eyes, there will come,—there must come, to every halt and lame and sick eye,—a renewal of childish health, a natural vigour and readiness to see every sight, to touch each part of our distantly whirling planet with the eye's meditative stalk.

FROM: DIVINE REVOLT

LEE'S RETURN

When sullied world is gone, or rent
Hidden meanings like hidden ghosts arise.
That Lee might live the thought fidelity,
To defeat or victory indifferent,
A world's measure of gain and loss
Lies in his swords' ceremonial cross.

O nothing but a passion burns
Mourned countries to their soot.

Spotless Appomattox first and last,
Lee's ruinous duty, and after
Kent's canon that shook the stocks,
Who served a sane, distracted Lear
Because he knew a royal soul was one
Human before humanity had come.

Long, long lay the shadows on the grass;
Uniformed men flit and pass.

How many of the undiscerning multitude
When Lee passed there had thought
The great grey face all gravity,
Stone blossom of a moral root.
What first might drive a man
To live an abstract thought?

O nothing but a passion burns
Mourned countries to their soot.

Courthouse shadows judge the field
Where Lee both tried and failed;
A lonely, exalted thought that still
Drives restless as a nail.
O How had Athens come and gone
Without one such man?

Long, long lay the shadows on the grass;
Uniformed men flit and pass.

FROM: ADORING THORNS

I write this to all the harried angels of the earth
This is no post-mortem, but a moment recalled, my Dear
How briefly was her face tilted to the heaven where I lived! Never had

another angel—so hungry to experience love, real love, terrifying love and its frightful freedoms—come to the cool harbour of my arms with such intensity screwed into her face. Her face itself was an angel's puzzle; the tripped electric gate St Peter shut. An alert and mobile majesty in those pale features and dark locks that perhaps only still photography or a 1920s black and white film could possibly capture. In life, her grins and winning compressions of her nose seemed too hectic to be believed—too rash and ecstatic to really be communicating from any, more static, core one was willing to call recognizably "human." But I also knew these faces in their slow-motion mode, their more belatedly loving and august character. Alone, and at her feet, I would watch the world wash over her face at the end of the day in complaint and exasperation until it seemed that all expression must vanish from those exhausted lips and ceilingward, nearly black, eyes. Within moments, however, she would grimace or resolutely sigh—shaking her head like a wet terrier and, perhaps, open her blood-alive lips again to say my name or breathe out through a self-indulgent smile untraced by any concern other than its own tired loveliness. These were treasured instants, which I now (how calmly!) recollect. My bitterness, my anxiety, my righteous self-defence of some imagined personal integrity ripping from me now as the world then fell from her looks. And then I remember a slight sound of water mingling with her sidelit countenance; some fountain where we sat out a midnight vigil, the waterlight of rose and blue coral; laughing in delight at the airy realness of the stone cherubs floating before us rises to mind and floats around me now somehow liquidly—the unviewable sandpaper of the sea our only backdrop. Here was passion and patience and regret for the thought of a future we then in-hearsed, burying our told wishes as if just so much weight of dust. The taste of dust stays with me; dust and water still mingle on my tongue.

FROM: SEVEN HEAVENS

From the T'ung Shu: The Coin Prediction

When the coin prediction faces south
you are in for it: unrelenting disaster.

Lawyers will take everything,
there is no chance of winning.
Terrible deeds approach you.

Applying for a new thing
you will lose what you have.
No job. No money. No place to go.
Travel is advisable.
Marriage unravels,
you will lose at your arraignment.
A missing person will not be found.
You will get no help from a nobleman,
and no visitors.

FROM: THE ROSE LASSO

You Stood Up

You stood up, and the world rose with you!
Astounding globe, charter of misty distances, held love!

From you, all things emitted their eternal energy.
From you, the sensual regale of lifted light, diamonds!

From you, spears of daybreak arose, laughing lioness!
Night abandoned melancholy, ropes of dew lifted with you.

Dark-headed iris of a thousand days,
When love comes before us we abandon everything.

FROM: XXX SONNETS

The unfair love that develops in a concentrated boy or girl for the
words of the dead—this is the central college experience. It makes us
harsh and discontent with our contemporaries. For how can the home
and dorm-bred cry lifted from behind a cheap desk compare with that

Shelleyian lilt and agony passing time has patinaed with an ineluctable grace? An institution of publishing, such as our small review, works against this cynicism—which every great creator has disposed of in his time—and permits the clear registration of value to enter the ear with the intent impact of a whisper. The page of a review is as serviceable a blank for our Elroy as for any England's Shelley. And the context of the times, which bookends such productions, does not subtract from the effort of any individual but rather lends its substance to the impact of a voice raised from amidst its mass.

FROM: THE CABANA AT THE EQUATOR

It was his mother's going, her poignant death,
Like still water, that made him hear
Curlicues of God's named trumpet world.
A French horn paddles in his ear;
Finches mocked the minister at her wake, his frown
Emitted solo labyrinths, corona icicles of round.
Tenor Semblance. leaving, knew his feet
Were tambourines, clashing in the grass.
And when he whispered, it was with sorrow
That he could not ring himself a barrow.
In her twinking time upon this mortal orb,
In laundered air, tender sequences
Of love and love, flashed from her bright center
Like perpetual suns that sang and knew their tune.
It was because of her he sought
A personal, vocal dew.

FROM: PROMETHEUS BOUND

P O W E R
We have slid a long way down, to earth's end.
Now we are in an arid gorge, close rocks
Hem our freedoms and our bruised feet have reached

The lowest place. Hephastos, turn your mind
That forged the golden playthings of the gods
To harsher endeavors; let invention
Wither, and let love's meaningless surplus
Be dried up. Have your ire flare again
In residence where he's made your flames vanish,
Putting out the light of goldenest craft
To help sprouting man, who rankly weeds
A gardened globe. Forge in violent fires
Bellowed large again by your oppressed heart
Thorned chains to lay him against these hard stones
In unmoving misery.

FROM: LOUIS B. LIPCHINTZ ABANDONS SHIP

A lighthearted children's tale fully illustrated with an ironical message for it adult auditors about the brevity a passing of all things beautiful....

FROM: DR. KILMER'S OCEAN-WEED HEART REMEDY

On my first trip to Europe, I killed a Gothic town. I was burning in the 121st regiment. It was just the other summer. Black in my wax-sheen wetsuit, I blew up a munitions factory with waterproofed dynamite. I hid behind the tread of a German tank some plastered church had swallowed. Holy glass lit up with the explosions. Job smiled beneath his multi-colored boils; the sinister sulk of the tank's sway-back body inherited his outlines: bright, abstract as flowers. I returned to the buoyant teardrop of the Mediterranean quietly as a cyclist.

With my light head half under water, the dark sea seemed to encircle the incinerated star of the town.

FROM: A CREDENT REGALE

a credent regale—rare back issue of the magazine that rocked the NYC poetry world

FROM: CORDIAL RENEGADES

"It needs work," Tear said to himself as blazen images soared his skull. He concealed himself by the door of a boutique and was looking through its neon scrawl as strains of droning distortion flowed from within. Tear loved coming to New York as it stimulated his reflective nature. All the irritation was gone as he thought of the scorch that his words would leave upon the world. Ambitions awoke within him as he thought of this noble mission. He could smell the leathers from inside the shop as ghosts from things past arose to haunt and crawl his brain. This tore him up, as these were the cruel winds that would always enervate his passions, like the browning leaf of St. Mark's that fell past his boot, wilting.

FROM: AUTOBIOGRAPHIES; ESSAYS AND INTRODUC-TIONS

WHENEVER I THINK of that woman, the great wreck of her life before me, I am moved, as it were, by a tangible nothingness. What the mind's eye cannot create it cannot devour; and there was nothing in those languorous limbs and dim hair darker than ravening midnight that had ever been in my brain before. All her gestures were the work of a noble indolence; all her thought a race in terror from the unjust atrocities of the world. Nothing was more beautiful, nor more foreign to my imagination than such a creature.

It was before a bough of May, and not a winter's branch, that I first saw her. She had in her eye some coin of sharp umber that flashed intermittently over whatever she passed by. On her body she wore a loose cloth of yellow-gold, under which she had safety-pinned together a bodice of lace, dark garters and a pair of cherry-red boxing shorts.

FROM: AUTOBIOGRAPHIES; DEUS ABSCONDIS

A light rain threatens as I whirl to a halt through fall leaves to the house-doorway of the deaf school and knock at number 206. The door is opened by Schnaebel, who I had thought was a student of the establishment, but is instead a curly balding 23 or 24 year old teacher there, the head of something or other. At a round table crowded with papers to my viewing right is a pudgy blonde woman who smiles at me, as if politely embarrassed for my sake that I interrupted such important work as they were doing.

FROM: THE DEATH OF SATAN

Selected poems 1988-1998

FROM: EVERLASTING ARCHANGELS

Poems of the New Romantics

FROM: ANTIGONE; SOPHOKLES RESSURECTED

ANTIGONE. Calamity's the great text
our sorrow-sighs must punctuate.
Sisters in misery, we fare not well
under a hard hail from Hell.
Who's got a better right to cry for vengeance?
The dead have lost their old intemperance
and lay in rotten equanimity all day—
it's us, we need someplace to throw our hearts away,
some bloody spot of ground to shout alone.
Soldiers and women both inter the bones;
but only women have no place to vent
the things with which their hearts are bent;

our heads of our greifs we can't delouse
while men make all the world a charnalhouse
and for their killing get crowned as Kings,
with ruby wands decreeing royal things.
We women in our low office may only weep;
unceasing calamity, Ismene, is ours to keep.
Oh, that of the royal house of Oedipus
I knew nothing, and cared less!
Topping it off, a rape has rasped my ears today,
sharp soot from the dragon's-mouth polluting lucidity,
dark words evilly twisting the clarity of air,
the few clear things we've scraped together
from the stark wreckage of our hates and hurts.

FROM: BURNING BYZANTIUM

An Annunciation
Drowned in the puling cradle emptiness has lit,
In empty action of a tragedian's strut
Hollow on a stage, a struggle in the sheets
Tosses some watery image up, toiling to be born.
What rose, with stolen bone or shafted ear,
Lash-astonished, oceanic there?
Was it some dragon-fantastic
Imago of a phaseless man, phantom-real,
Or a sea-struck Hamlet's ghostly father,
Rising out of night to the topmost walk
When all the mind's aroused?
Those dying eyes in a face blood-suffused
Scan the gathered stares of men, new-ignited
Out of an age's hesitations, dying to be born.

About the Author

Gregg Glory [Gregg G. Brown] is the founder of BLAST PRESS [**http://www.corporategreed.com/gregglory**], the ONLY LITER-ARY PRESS IN EXISTENCE!!!!! He may be contacted at **gregglory@aol.com**. He is busy writing poetry.

0-595-23097-0

Printed in the United States
111088LV00003B/69/A